Mail Order Mate

Book 47 in Brides of Beckham

Kirsten Osbourne

Chapter One

Kate Jessup stood waiting until the ladies at the front of the store cleared, so she could purchase the fabric she'd found for dresses for some of her clients. Thanks to her friend Florence, her business was booming, and she was pleased to be able to make dresses for the wealthy ladies in town, even though they wouldn't ever speak with her in public.

She and her fiancé had anticipated their wedding vows by just a week, but when her fiancé had died the day before they were meant to be married, she was left pregnant and alone. His twin brother had helped her out as much as he could, but it just didn't seem right to take anything from Jake.

She'd named her three-year-old son, Jesse, and he went everywhere she did, even when she was purchasing fabric. Instead of looking toward the front of the store like she was ready to check out, she stared at the bulletin board in the back of the store. She spotted an ad for mail-order brides and couldn't help but smile. Her friend, Florence, had moved to Cheyenne and married her late fiancé's brother Jake, using that exact agency.

She stared at it for a moment, wondering if she could contact the agency herself. She didn't know if having a son born out of wedlock would disqualify her, but she decided to try. Why not? Her only stipulation would be staying in Cheyenne where her clients and her friends were. Not that she had more than Florence and Jake as friends, but that didn't matter too terribly much. Friends were friends, and she adored the couple.

She took down the notice and put it into her reticule before going to the front of the store, now that the ladies who spoke ill of her had left. "Hello, Mr. Jorgensen."

"Hello there, Miss Jessup. More fabric?" he asked, taking the yard goods from her. "Business must be booming."

"Oh, it is! Thanks to Mrs. Weatherby. She was the first to wear one of my dresses, and now all of the ladies in town want an original."

"Good for you!" he said. "I'm impressed by how hard you've worked to get to where you are." The kindly store owner took a peppermint stick and handed it to Jesse.

Jesse smiled, sticking the candy into his mouth.

"What do you say to Mr. Jorgensen?"

Jesse removed the peppermint stick. "Thank you."

"You're welcome, Jesse!"

After Kate had paid for the order, she left the store, thinking of the ad in her reticule. Maybe she was crazy to even think about it, but she wanted to find someone who could make her happy, like her fiancé Jesse had.

When she got to the tiny <u>house</u> she shared with Jesse, she put him down for his nap, and then went to the table where she quickly wrote a letter to the matchmaker. She explained her situation, not glossing over the fact that her reputation was terrible due to Jesse's birth. Instead, she explained what had happened and how very much she loved her son and wanted to stay in Cheyenne.

She'd mail the letter in the morning, praying that Mrs. Elizabeth Tandy could find her a hero for her own love story.

EMMETT WHITAKER WAS taking photos of the town of Beckham, Massachusetts, when the telegram caught up with him. His father had died, and he needed to head home to take the reins on the ranch where he'd grown up. He sat on the only chair available, a rocking chair in front of the town mercantile, and rubbed his hands over his face.

He and his father had been close until his mother, a woman who knew better and more than everyone around her, had chased him away. It didn't help that the young lady he'd been eyeing since they'd been in school together was engaged to another man. His mother's gossipy ways had made him never want to be in or around Cheyenne again.

But he didn't have a choice anymore. Back to Cheyenne he must go, and he would take over his family's business. He'd always known the years he was on his own, going from place to place to photograph different towns, wouldn't last long.

He sighed, looking down at his camera, and wishing it wouldn't be the last time he held it. He was proud of what he'd accomplished as a photographer, and he only expected his mother would be just as proud of what he'd done.

A tall blond man stopped beside him. "Are you all right, sir?"

Emmett nodded. "I am. Mostly."

The man studied him for a moment. "You need a good meal. Come to my house for supper tonight." He gave him his address, and Emmett finally nodded.

"I'll be there."

"Six. No later, or you'll miss out." The blond man's eyes danced in merriment.

"I'll be there at five minutes til six then!"

"Smart man."

After those few words, the man disappeared into the store, and though Emmett realized he didn't know the man's name, he decided to go to supper. It would be his last night to eat supper away from home, if he didn't count the meals he would eat on the train. He would please himself. No one else truly mattered.

He went to the blond man's house and was there just before six. When he knocked, he was surprised that the man answered the door himself. Judging by the size and grandness of the house, he was certain the man had a very important job. What the job was, he didn't know, but he knew it had to be a good one.

He was led inside to an informal dining room, and he sat with the man and his wife. "I'm Emmett Whitaker."

The man smiled. "I guess we should have exchanged names earlier. I'm Bernard Tandy, and this is my wife, Elizabeth."

"You have a beautiful home," Emmett said.

"Thank you!" Mrs. Tandy replied. "What are you doing here in Beckham?"

"I'm a photographer, and I've been doing my best to document the growth in the smaller cities of the US that I believe has been caused by the railroad."

"How fascinating!"

Bernard smiled. "Shall I have the maid bring the food in?"

"That would be wonderful," Emmett said.

Left alone with Elizabeth for a moment, she smiled at him. "Is it terrible that I have no idea what we're having for supper tonight?" she asked.

He smiled. "Not at all. I'm glad your husband happened by me today. I had just received news of my father's death and my need to return to Cheyenne, Wyoming, to take over his ranch. I grew up knowing the ranch would be mine someday, but I didn't expect it this soon."

"I'm so sorry for your loss," Elizabeth said. "Do you still have people in Cheyenne?"

"My mother is still there, but I'm afraid we're not close."

"I'm so sorry. Would you like me to see if I can send you a bride?" she asked. "I'm a matchmaker and send mail-order brides to men in the west."

"What a fascinating career choice!" Emmett said. "Let me think on it."

She nodded. "I do have a woman in Cheyenne looking to marry, but she doesn't want to leave the area. If you're interested, we could make it happen rather easily. But please don't feel pressured. Today has been rough for you already, and you don't need someone shoving a new bride down your throat."

Emmett smiled. "Thank you for understanding that. I'm not certain why Mr. Tandy singled me out for a supper invitation, but I will say, it's just what I needed today."

"He said you looked sad, and he wanted to help you not be sad."

"I felt sad, so it would make sense that I looked sad as well."

Bernard returned to the dining room and took the seat at the head of the table, while Elizabeth sat at the foot. Emmett was sitting in the middle between them. "I thank you both for the supper invitation."

As they ate and shared small talk, Emmett couldn't quit thinking about what it would be like to have a wife. Someone who could serve as a buffer between him and his mother. It made sense that he would need a wife to bear children who would someday inherit the ranch.

Besides, he was expected to mingle with the upper echelons of Cheyenne society. It would be best if he had a wife who could muddle through it with him. He realized that both of the Tandys were watching him, as if they were expecting him to say something. "I'll take the mail-order bride," he said.

The words brought confusion to his host, but a smile from his hostess. "I'll help you with it after supper. She said she was ready to marry anytime, but it would be important to live somewhere other than her small home."

"Do you know her name?"

Elizabeth nodded. "I do. It might be more fun to be surprised, though, seeing as you both grew up there."

Emmett grinned, nodding. He couldn't help but think of sweet Kate Jessup, but he knew she had long since married Jesse. They probably had a couple of children by now. He'd been sweet on her since the moment he'd laid eyes on her though. He had simply been too shy to convey his feelings before Jesse Weatherby, the banker's son, had swooped in and made her fall in love with him.

After supper, he sat in Mrs. Tandy's office and answered her questions. When he was finished, he asked if he should send a telegram. "I don't think so. I'll send one to her, and have her wait at the train station in Cheyenne. I'm sure it will all work out just fine."

The next morning, Emmett boarded a train to return to Cheyenne, but in his mind, he kept envisioning Kate at the train station waiting for him. It would be nice to see her familiar face and sweet smile. Why, every time he thought about Cheyenne, her face popped into his head. To him, she and Cheyenne meant the same thing. Home.

ON THE MORNING OF HER wedding, Kate woke up later than usual, and she was exhausted. Jesse had been up half the night with a cough, and there was no one else to be with him. Now that she was making more money at her seamstress business, she would occasionally hire someone to mind him, but she still felt that she was his only parent, and therefore, the responsibility of raising the boy was all her own.

She decided to make a detour on the way to the train station and beg her friend Florence to watch him for a few hours. She hated to leave her son when he was sick, but what else was she to do? She was getting married that afternoon, and Jesse would be underfoot anyway.

Florence opened her door herself, her belly well-rounded with the child she carried. "Jesse was fussy all night and has a bit of a cough. Do you think you could care for him while I get married?"

"Of course, I'll take care of my sweet nephew. In fact, leave him here for a couple of nights while you two get married and get to know one another."

Kate's eyes widened. "I didn't bring extra clothes for him."

"We'll manage, even if I spend all day whipping up a long shirt for him to run about the house in."

"You really don't mind?"

Florence smiled. "Not at all. You need to get to know that man you're marrying and let him know that Jesse is well cared for." She picked him up out of his pram. "If he gets sicker, I'll send for the doctor."

Kate smiled, nodding. "Thank you so much. I can't believe how kind you are. I never expected it from you."

"Once I knew the truth, it was easy to love you both. Now go get married. Best wishes!"

Kate left the baby carriage there. She rarely used it for Jesse these days, but he was fussy this morning, having had as little sleep as she had. As she walked, she thought about her first impression of Florence.

Jake, the brother of the man she'd almost married, had told her that Florence believed the rumors that were going around town about Jake and Kate. He told her that Florence hadn't given him a chance to explain and had completely rejected him.

When she'd met Florence the following day at the mercantile, she'd thrown some candy at Florence. She had called her some names and told her she didn't deserve such a good man in her life. Florence had followed her home and had her explain everything.

As soon as Florence had understood that nothing had ever happened between Kate and Jake, she'd done everything she could to befriend her, going as far as to order a completely new wardrobe she hadn't needed, simply so she could show off Kate's dress designs.

Kate had thought about telling her not to waste her money, but she knew Jake could afford it, and she planned to pay her back for her time as soon as her business was doing a brisk enough business, which was very soon. She'd already stashed enough money that she could almost do it.

Chapter Two

Kate arrived at the train station just as the train pulled in. She waited patiently, nervously, for the mystery man who was from Cheyenne, who had agreed to marry her, knowing she had a son. She couldn't imagine a man that kind in the entire town except for maybe Jake. She'd been looked down on for so long that it was ridiculous.

As she watched, many familiar people got off the train, including an old school chum. They had never really been close, but she'd liked him a great deal. He was always respectful and never pulled pranks on the girls. He was a good man.

Spotting him, she decided to stroll over and welcome him home. She knew he'd been gone from Cheyenne for a while, but his father had recently died. That was probably why he was home. To take over his father's ranch.

She raised a hand in greeting as she approached Emmett. "Hello, stranger! It feels as if you've been gone forever."

Emmett smiled. "Kate! I wasn't expecting to see you as soon as I stepped off the train. What are you doing here?"

Kate blushed. "I'm waiting for a man that a matchmaker sent me."

"Not Elizabeth Tandy?" he asked, staring at her. This was too good to be true. Elizabeth had matched him up with his dream girl? At her slow nod, he grinned. "Let me introduce myself then. I'm your future husband."

Kate blinked a few times. "Really? Have you talked to your mother about this?"

"My mother has nothing to do with the person I marry. I don't know why you would think she does."

Kate bit her lip. "We should sit and talk for a minute before you rush into marriage with me."

Emmett frowned. "I know you have a son. That doesn't bother me. Jesse passed?"

She nodded. "Yes, the day *before* our wedding." She stressed the word before, so he would know she had never married. Surely that would make him realize she wasn't the right bride for him.

He blinked once, then nodded. "I see." If it had been anyone else in the world, he'd have thought a little less of her. "Where's your son now?" He'd expected the boy to be there with them.

"He's got a bit of a cough, so his aunt is watching him. We do not need a cranky three-year-old at our wedding."

"I was looking forward to meeting him. Are you ready for the wedding?" he asked, picking up two bags, one of which looked like it was really heavy by the way he lifted it.

She frowned. "You're still going to marry me? Your mother absolutely abhors me, and she thinks I'm the worst person in the world because my child is a bastard." She said the last word, even though she'd never let it be said about her son.

"Of course, I am. I know you, Kate Jessup. I know that you're one of the best people I've ever met, and I don't care what my mother thinks of you." He frowned. "Though maybe we should have our wedding night at your place and put off telling my mother I'm home for a couple of days."

She laughed. "Seriously?"

He nodded. "Why not? I've known you my whole life. I know you don't make a habit of having children out of wedlock."

She smiled at that. "No one does."

"Well, then, what do I have to complain about?" He didn't exactly like that she had an illegitimate child, but he was more open-minded than his mother. Besides, he'd have been willing to follow her anywhere as a boy, and that feeling didn't seem to have gone away.

They went to the church and were married quickly. When the pastor told him he could kiss his bride, it was all he could do not to shout in celebration. What could be better than being married to Kate? He reached for her, and pulled her into his arms, his mouth coming down on hers in a kiss he'd dreamed about for years.

Kate was stunned when the kiss he gave her at the wedding was as passionate as she'd ever felt. She'd expected a quick peck on the lips, but it was so much more than that. She quickly lost herself, forgetting that they were in church and standing in front of the pastor. Emmett's kiss was spectacular.

Finally, the pastor cleared his throat, and Emmett broke off the kiss, mumbling, "Sorry, Pastor."

"Quite all right!"

Emmett caught Kate's hand in his and left the church with her after paying the pastor. As they walked, he couldn't stop grinning at her. "That was some kiss," she said softly.

He chuckled. "Sorry. I forgot where we were for a moment."

Having thought she would dread her husband's attention Kate was happy they'd kissed that way. Now she knew she would love it when he touched her, and she wanted to grab his hand and drag him to her house. "Have you eaten?" she asked, thinking about what she had to feed him.

He nodded. "Is that little restaurant still on this street?"

She nodded, though she hadn't eaten there since her parents had left her. "Yes, it is. I've heard it's better than ever."

"Then let's have lunch and celebrate that neither of us married a stranger today like we thought we would when we woke."

She smiled and nodded. He was right. She did feel like celebrating that it had been Emmett at the train station and not a stranger. "I hope you won't mind if I continue working," she said. She'd once thought her life would be perfect when she was marrying Jesse, but how strange it had ended up. She'd gone from being the daughter of a well-off couple to being the mother of a boy and being scorned by all the people of town. No, she'd make sure she could always support herself because she had to be able to take care of her little boy.

While seated at the restaurant, he noticed the waitress wrinkled her nose at Kate. Just a little, but it gave him an idea of how the townspeople had treated her after giving birth to her son. After ordering, he took her hand in his, looking down at how delicate her fingers looked. "I don't mind if you want to keep working. What do you do?"

She smiled. "I'm a seamstress. Ladies who won't even look at me because I'm beneath them, now wear my gowns."

"I'm surprised they do!" Emmett was well aware of how judgmental people could be.

"It's a recent development actually. Do you remember Jesse's twin brother, Jake?"

"Oh, of course. Jake Weatherby is a good man!"

"He is. Well, Jake got married in the late summer of last year. His wife is who is watching little Jesse today. Anyway, when she moved to town, she assumed I'd slept with Jake as that was the rumor that had been floating about town for years. I gave her a piece of my mind in a not so ladylike fashion. When she realized that I told the truth, and Jesse wasn't Jake's son, she hired me to make her a whole new wardrobe. Now, she'd just gotten married, and already had a new wardrobe, but she wanted to help me so she paid to make that happen. Then she wore my dresses around town, telling everyone who would listen that I'd made them."

Emmett blinked, a slow grin crossing his face. "And since Jake is well-known as the richest man in town, everyone wanted to emulate his wife."

Kate nodded. "I could not have paid for such a wonderful advertising campaign. Within weeks I had women lining up at my door to hire me."

"That's fabulous!" He was pleased to hear that she'd had it a bit easier lately. "And now they all should acknowledge you as an equal. Now that we're married."

"I don't think it's going to be quite so easy. Your mother...well, she holds a prominent position socially, and the other women won't go against her. And she hates me. Loathes me. Despises me."

"I'm sure it's not that bad. I'm also sure, I'll gladly spend my wedding night away from her, so she can say nothing against you."

Kate smiled a bit. As much as she knew her life would be better with Emmett as her husband, she also knew how very badly his mother had treated her. She was truly nervous about the moment the older woman found out that she was her new daughter-in-law.

After lunch, they held hands as they walked back to her home, and she was thankful she'd spent as much time tidying up as she had the day before. Her home was still a bit of a mess with all of the fabric she had lying about, but it didn't look dirty.

Once inside, he took her into his arms and kissed her again. She frowned. "It's not even dark out!"

He chuckled. "It doesn't need to be dark."

"Are you sure?" she asked.

"Trust me."

This time when he lowered his mouth to hers, she wrapped her arms around him and kissed him back for all she was worth. Maybe she wasn't in love with him, but he made her body feel things that she'd never felt before.

When his hand went to the buttons at the back of her dress, she didn't protest, wanting him out of his clothes as well. She unbuttoned his shirt, even as he unbuttoned her dress, and she pulled it off his shoulders. She could feel that the buttons were not sewn on well, and she promised herself she'd take on the task of making his shirts for him.

When he pulled her dress off her shoulders and she felt it pool at her feet, she didn't let herself take the time to be embarrassed at her nudity, and went straight back into his arms.

His hands roamed over the flesh he'd uncovered, and though she still wore her corset and petticoat, it felt as if he had touched every inch of her flesh. She trembled, and felt her body lit on fire by his touch.

"Turn around so I can get this blasted corset off you!" he said. "Women should not be forced to wear these things."

"I hate them," she admitted as she turned, and he untied her corset strings.

"Never wear one again," he said.

She couldn't agree to such a thing, so she kept silent, waiting as he pushed the offensive garment to the floor at her feet. While he was at it, he removed her petticoat, and it joined all the other clothing on the floor.

She stood before him, naked except for her drawers, and he smiled. "You look exactly like I've always imagined."

The words seemed odd to her as he said them, but she couldn't put her finger on why. Not with all the passion she was feeling toward this man, her childhood friend.

When she was completely undressed, he scooped her up in his arms. "Where's the bedroom?" he asked.

She pointed in the direction of her room, and he carried her there, slowly lowering her to the bed. He took a moment to finish removing his own clothes before he followed her down.

It never occurred to her that he was moving too quickly, because she wanted everything he did to her. When he laid down beside her on the bed and began stroking all of her sensitive spots, she moaned softly, amazed at how quickly he roused a part of herself she'd thought was dormant.

When his body covered hers and he joined them as one, she gasped but wrapped her arms and legs around him and held on tight. Never had she imagined having a man inside her could feel this good.

As her fulfillment came upon her, she arched her back and cried out his name, giving him the knowledge he needed to drive himself to find the same blessed place she was in.

He rolled from her and lay beside her, still unable to stop his hands from roaming over her body and toying with her nipples. He kissed her again, this time it was a softer kiss and much gentler than his earlier kisses had been. "You are everything I've always dreamed of and more, Kate Whitaker," he said.

"That was pretty wonderful for me as well," she replied. "It's nice to have some time alone before your mother makes us both miserable."

He frowned. "Are you that worried about my mother?"

"You haven't seen how she's treated me these last few years. It's been really bad, and all of the other women in town followed her lead."

"What about your mother? She doesn't defend you?"

She closed her eyes for a moment. "Not since I told her I was pregnant. She and Father even moved back east so they wouldn't be embarrassed by me."

"That's really sad. You've been totally alone."

Kate shook her head. "I've had Jesse's brother on my side the whole time. When I had any money troubles he was there to help. He's a really good man."

"It sounds like it. I didn't really know either Jesse or Jake. I need to get to know him."

Kate nodded. "He's the only banker in town, so you'll be doing business with him if nothing else. But he is little Jesse's uncle so we will have lots of contact with them."

"You don't mind letting him stay there, obviously. I think it's good you're keeping him in touch with his father's family as much as you can."

"I agree. And his new auntie loves him something fierce. I can't wait for you to meet Florence. She's a wonderful woman."

"I'll look forward to meeting her then. We'll have to have her and Jake over for supper sometime soon."

"As long as your mother doesn't kick me out of the house," she said.

"My mother doesn't have the authority to kick you out of the house. I know my father, and he put me as his sole heir, knowing I'd take care of her. She has no rights as far as you're concerned."

Kate nodded, but she had a feeling it wasn't going to go as smoothly as he'd said. She was one of the few ladies in town who hadn't switched to her for seamstress services.

As they laid there in bed in the middle of the afternoon, they caught up on what they'd done for the past few years. "I knew you'd left town, but I didn't know why."

Emmett sighed. "Part of it was I couldn't bear to deal with my mother any longer. She had an opinion of everyone I ever thought about courting and all my friends. I needed to stand on my own two feet for a while. And I found a love of photography. I've been traveling around this great country of ours, snapping photographs of different small towns. I came back because my father died, and it's time for me to do what life demands of me, and not traveling around taking photographs."

"Do you still have your equipment?" she asked.

"Of course. Why?"

"I wouldn't mind some portraits of our family or even just of Jesse. I love the idea of having a photo of him at this age, so I won't have to forget exactly how he looked."

Emmett nodded. "I can do that easily."

"Oh, you should get one of Jake's wife as well. She's expecting and nice and round. She wouldn't like it much, but I know that her husband would."

"And her name is Florence? Is that what you said?"

Kate nodded. "Good memory. What made you decide to see a matchmaker?"

He smiled. "I was sitting on a bench in front of the general store in Beckham, Massachusetts right after I received the telegram about my father's death. This nice man stopped and talked to me on his way into the mercantile, and he invited me to supper. Not wanting to be alone right after finding out my father died, I agreed to supper with them. His wife is the matchmaker you wrote to. She talked to me that night, and I agreed, not wanting to have to live alone with my mother. I figured a wife could be a buffer between us."

She laughed. "Not sure what kind of a buffer I'll be."

"We'll stand united."

Chapter Three

Emmett and Kate spent two full days hiding out in her small house before they collected Jesse and went to the ranch where he'd grown up. It only took a moment for the boy to make Emmett smile, and he was sure he'd love the boy with his whole heart.

"How old are you?" Emmett asked.

Jesse held up three fingers. "I'm three!"

Kate smiled. "He'll be four next month. It's hard to believe he's been the whole focus of my life for so long."

Florence stood behind Jesse smiling. "He was so good for me. The cough hasn't been bad at all."

"Oh good. I'm surprised Mrs. Andrews let you spend any time with him at all!"

"Me too! I had to beg a few times, and she wouldn't let him eat meals with us, but for the most part, she took care of him. You know how she is."

Kate looked at Emmett. "Mrs. Andrews is their housekeeper. She raised Jesse and Jake after their parents were killed."

"I guess I never knew that. I think it's great that he gets to spend time with her then."

Jesse looked at Emmett. "Are you my new pa?"

Kate held her breath, having no idea how Emmett would respond to such a question. "I am. Do you want to ride out to the wagon on my shoulders?" Emmett had left her home the day before to buy two horses and a wagon. He knew his mother would have plenty for them to use, but he bought these with the money he'd earned as a photographer, which made him feel like they were truly his own.

Jesse nodded excitedly. "Uncle Jake lets me ride on his shoulders."

"Well, it sounds like your Uncle Jake is a pretty terrific man. Do you like to be here?"

"Yes!" Jesse yelled.

Kate eyed her son. "We don't yell in the house."

Jesse had the manners to look contrite. "Yes, ma'am."

Florence's lips were twitching which made Kate want to laugh as well, so instead she narrowed her eyes at her friend. "Thank you for having Jesse for a visit. I'm sure I'll have to unspoil him."

"Speaking of which…" Florence produced a suitcase that was rather heavy. She gave it to Kate with a sheepish look. "I didn't feel like sewing, so I took him shopping instead."

Kate shook her head. "And how many toys did he talk you into buying?" she asked.

Florence just shrugged. "As many as were necessary."

Kate hugged Florence. "You have to quit spoiling him!"

"At the moment, he's the only child in my life. Of course, I have to spoil him!"

Kate shook her head. "I'll see you Sunday."

"Why don't you come over for Sunday dinner with us after church?"

Kate looked at Emmett who smiled. "I want to get to know you and Jake. Sounds like the perfect time."

"What's your last name?" Florence asked, realizing Kate hadn't used it when introducing him.

He sighed. "Whitaker."

"I do believe I know your mother." Florence didn't show anything about how she felt about his mother as she said the words.

"I'm sure you do." He grinned. "We're going to take our son now, and head out to the ranch. She doesn't know I'm back in town yet."

"Then I'm glad you had a couple of days before you had to present your new family to her."

"Me too!" he said, as he headed for the door. As soon as they were out, Emmett swung Jesse up onto his shoulders and carried him out to the wagon. "Now, do you want to ride on your ma's lap or do you want to ride in the back?"

Jesse looked excited to have the choice. "I want to ride in the back!"

Kate was a bit hesitant, but finally she agreed. "You be careful. I don't want to go over a bump and see you fly out of the back of the wagon."

Jesse giggled. "I'll be good."

All of Kate and Jesse's belongings were in the back of the wagon, and Jesse stood right behind the seat, between Emmett and Kate. "Are we going home now?" he asked.

"Do you remember when I told you we were going to move to wherever your new daddy lived?"

Jesse nodded.

"Well, he's taking us to his house now."

"Oh." Jesse seemed to understand it was something exciting.

As they drove, Emmett told Kate not to worry about his mother. "I'll take care of her."

Kate nodded, but she really did know better. Emmett would have no way to convince his mother that Kate and Jesse belonged in their home.

When they pulled up outside the large ranch house that Emmett had grown up in, he hurried around and helped her down. "It's all going to be fine. I need you to remember that."

Kate smiled sweetly, taking Jesse's suitcase from the back of the wagon, and holding the hand of her son as they approached the house. "Does she even know you were getting married?"

Emmett shook his head. "No, but she will soon."

He strode ahead of them to the house and went inside, not holding the door for Kate. She wasn't surprised though. He would need to say a few words to his mother first. She waited on the front porch swing while he talked to her, pulling Jesse up with her to sit.

If Jesse wondered why they hadn't gone inside, he didn't ask, and Kate didn't offer the information. What difference would it make?

Emmett came back out ten minutes later. "Sorry to leave you two out here. Come in."

When Kate stepped foot in his house for the first time, she felt as if she was coming home, and it was an odd feeling. Of course, her parents' house had been very much like his. They'd been ranchers who lived a short distance from the Whitakers.

It only took a minute for Mrs. Whitaker to walk into the entrance hall and see Kate and Jesse. "It's bad enough that you married without telling me, but to her? She's a whore!"

Kate smiled at Mrs. Whitaker, not denying her words, which she'd been hearing the woman use for years about her. "It's good to see you again, Mrs. Whitaker."

"You will not call my wife names in her own house!" Emmett said, already fed up with his mother, and he'd only been home for a few minutes. "She is the mistress of this house now, and you're the mother-in-law. No bad names!"

Mrs. Whitaker's eyes narrowed. "But you just brought your whore and her bastard to live with me. What are you thinking? This ranch needs a strong man to run it, not some pushover who doesn't think it's a bad idea to marry a woman no one else would have."

Kate turned to Emmett, seeing that his face was red with anger. "Why don't you show me to our room and to Jesse's? I can start putting things away."

Emmett led the way upstairs, where he showed her a small bedroom that had a big bed. "Mother says this is our room for now. I thought she'd give us the master bedroom, but when she looked outside and saw you and Jesse, she lost her mind."

Kate nodded, smiling a little. "I'm not surprised. It's all right. We can manage."

Emmett was disgusted with how his mother had treated his new wife, but he knew the only way around it would be to lay low for a little while.

Emmett quickly began bringing in their belongings from the wagon, while Kate and Jesse looked at their rooms and unpacked their things. "Have you had lunch yet?" Kate finally asked her son. At his nod, she smiled. "I think it's naptime then."

Jesse dragged his feet, but he was asleep almost as soon as his head hit the pillow. As much as he dreaded sleeping, he needed his naps more than most children she knew.

Finally, Emmett finished carrying everything inside. "I need to go and see how the ranch is doing. Get my bearings all over again. I know my father has done some expanding, and I need to know just how many men he has working for him. I need to get an idea of what I'm jumping into." He kissed her softly. "I'll be back in a couple of hours."

Kate nodded, smiling at him. "I hope all goes well." After he was gone, she put away the last of her belongings before going downstairs, knowing his mother would be there, but not wanting to see her. "Would you like me to fix supper tonight?"

Mrs. Whitaker glared at her. "It's my son's first night at home in years. The fact that you're here to spoil it is enough. I'll make supper."

Kate nodded. "I'll go upstairs and do some of my work then." She didn't wait to hear what Mrs. Whitaker had to say about that. There was no reason. She would do what she needed to do and do her best not to be upset by the harridan.

Going back upstairs, Kate took out a dress she was making for one of the women in town. Her fingers flew as she sewed the silk dress together, knowing she needed to add the little bit of embroidery her customer wanted to the collar. She prided herself on the little touches she made to each dress. No two were ever alike, even if they were made in the same style. She made certain of that.

As soon as the dress was finished, she went to work on the flowers for the collar, keeping herself upstairs as long as she could.

The smell of fresh bread was in the air, and Kate wished she'd eaten before they left their little house in town. She'd made a sandwich for Emmett, but she'd been too nervous to be hungry. Now she was sitting with her stomach growling at her as she finished the dress in front of her.

Jesse woke and cried, not remembering where he was. She went to him and held him for a bit. "I'm working. Can you play quietly?"

Jesse was used to being asked to play while she worked, but normally, he was allowed to make noise. "Yes, ma'am."

She left her door open, so Jesse could come to her if he needed to as she finished up the delicate work of the flowers.

As soon as she was done with the dress, she started on the matching hat. She didn't usually work as a milliner, but this particular customer had wanted a hat that was made of the same silk as the dress. It was easy enough to manage.

She had just finished and gone to check on Jesse when Emmett came inside. He was filthy, and she smiled. "I hope you know where the bathtub is!"

He laughed, nodding. "But I have to kiss you first!"

She squealed as she jumped away from him, and Jesse got between the two of them. He pointed his finger at his new pa, and said, "You have to be nice to my mama!"

Kate laughed. "He's just teasing me, Jesse. It's all right."

Jesse gave one last narrow-eyed look to Emmett before he returned to playing with his wooden train his Aunt Florence had purchased for him. Kate had been quite surprised at all the new toys, but she hadn't said anything. She knew her friend liked to spoil Jesse.

While Emmett took his bath, Kate got Jesse cleaned up for supper. She had no idea how Mrs. Whitaker would expect Jesse to look for the meal, but she wasn't taking any chances on the woman spewing more vitriol on her son.

Emmett walked into the bedroom, freshly washed and wearing clean clothes. "I didn't know if we were expected to dress for supper," she said.

"Oh, you look beautiful as you are. And look how handsome Jesse looks with his hair combed."

Kate smiled, pleased that he'd complimented her son as well as her. "We're ready then."

"Mother said supper was ready," he said, offering Kate his arm.

Jesse went downstairs before Kate and followed his nose to the food. Kate quickened her step because Jesse didn't need to be mistreated for her actions. "What are you cooking?"

Mrs. Whitaker looked over her shoulder to see the boy. "Roast beef. My baby just came home from being gone for a very long time."

Jesse looked around. "Who's your baby?"

"Emmett. He's my son!"

"Does that mean you're my grandma?" he asked.

"Heavens no! Where would you get an idea like that?"

"Emmett said he's my pa now, and if you're his ma, then you're my grandma," Jesse patiently explained.

Mrs. Whitaker glared at Kate, who had walked up behind her son. "What would you like for Jesse to call you, Mrs. Whitaker?"

"He may call me Mrs. Whitaker."

Kate nodded, smiling down at Jesse. "She's to be called Mrs. Whitaker, not Grandma."

"But...I want to call her Grandma."

Kate shook her head. "She doesn't like that name."

Jesse looked confused, but he nodded. "Yes, ma'am."

Emmett scooped Jesse up and carried him to the table, setting him on one side, right smack in the middle.

For a moment, Kate tried to decide where to sit, but she chose to sit across from Jesse, so she could help him with his food and allow Mrs. Whitaker to sit at the foot of the table, where she knew the older woman would prefer to be.

Emmett frowned as he noticed her take the spot, but he said nothing. He didn't want to have their first argument as man and wife in front of his mother and their son.

When Mrs. Whitaker joined them, Kate said, "Since you were kind enough to cook for all of us, I hope you'll allow me to do the dishes."

Mrs. Whitaker nodded, as if she was doing a favor for Kate. "I'll allow it."

Emmett wanted to say something, but he knew it would be better if he talked to his mother about the way she treated Kate privately instead of saying something in front of Kate and Jesse. And he had a lot to say to his mother about how she was treating Kate.

His wife was going to have a place of honor in their home, and his mother was going to have to deal with it. When he prayed over the meal, he thanked God for bringing Kate and Jesse into his life and making him so happy. After he raised his head, he could see in his mother's face that she'd taken his words as a declaration of war. Not that he minded. He refused to choose his mother over his wife. It would never be all right.

Chapter Four

When Kate woke the following morning, she noticed that Emmett was already up and probably getting ready to work. When she peeked in at Jesse, he was still sound asleep, so Kate hurried down the stairs as soon as she was dressed.

Unfortunately, when she reached the bottom of the stairs, she heard Mrs. Whitaker yelling at Emmett. "I told you, I don't want that woman living under my roof. She has no moral values!"

"I'm not going to argue about this for another minute. I'm going to go out and milk the cows and gather the eggs. If you don't want her under the same roof as you, I do know there's a cabin that Grandmother and Granddaddy lived in before they built this house. I can have it fixed up for you within a day or two."

Upon hearing the threat, Kate covered her mouth with her hand. As much as she thought Julie Whitaker was a busybody, who needed to pay attention to herself for a while, she didn't want the older woman to be tossed out on her ear. She could only imagine how horrible that would be.

She stepped into the kitchen, pretending she hadn't heard a word. "Would you like me to fix breakfast, Mrs. Whitaker?" she asked, smiling at the older woman.

"No, I do not want you cooking in my kitchen. Knowing you, you'll set the whole thing on fire!"

Kate nodded, still smiling, though it was much harder now. "Then I'll go collect the eggs. I've never been a lazy woman, and if you won't let me help in the kitchen, then I'll have to find another way to help."

"Stop smiling at me!" Mrs. Whitaker yelled. "I think you are disgusting, and I don't want you here, and you keep smiling at me as if you don't know what else to do with your face!"

Kate felt her lips twitching in another smile, but she was able to control herself. As much as the woman hated her, she was torturing them both. "All right." She plucked the egg basket off the counter, and went outside to find eggs, knowing that Emmett was right beside her.

As soon as they were in the barn, and he was certain they were out of earshot of the house, he shook his head. "Stop being nice to her. She treats you like you're dung on her shoes!"

"I know she does. And she hates it when I smile at her. So I'll keep smiling. It's my little twist of the knife."

He gaped at her for a moment before throwing his head back and laughing. "I like the way you see things."

She took a step closer to him and put her palms flat on his chest. "And I like the way you look." Standing on tiptoe, she kissed him. "Too bad it's daylight. I kind of prefer our night time activities."

He grinned at that. "You're not the only one." Grasping her waist, he pulled her flush up against him and kissed her. The kiss made them both forget about his mother and the work to be done.

After a long while, she broke off the kiss, looking around her. "Your kisses make me forget everything. Jesse will be up soon. I need to gather the eggs and get in there before he runs into your mother when he looks for me."

Emmett groaned. "How on earth did I think this was going to be all right?"

She shrugged. "We probably shouldn't have married. I expected this all along."

"No, we should have married. My mother just needs to learn some manners."

"She probably does. But I'm not going to be the one to teach them to her. I refuse to add to the chaos in the house. I'll keep smiling and doing as she says and pretending nothing she has to say against me hurts in any way."

"But it does hurt, doesn't it?"

"Well, of course. It's hard to have someone call you a whore and not be hurt." She kissed him once more. "I'm collecting eggs. You do the milking. We'll meet back inside. Maybe your mother will go away for a while this afternoon. Wouldn't that be nice?"

He couldn't help but grin, enjoying the view as she walked away from him. He was married to the most beautiful woman on earth, and he needed to make sure he remembered that fact.

Kate spent the next little while gathering eggs, and when she approached the house, she heard voices. She wanted to cry. Jesse had gone looking for her and found Mrs. Whitaker.

She stopped for a moment on the porch. "Mrs. Whit— are you sure I can't call you Grandma? That's so much easier to say than your name."

"I'm positive," Mrs. Whitaker said. But as Kate peeked in the window, she saw Emmett's mother give Jesse a cookie. "Now go sit at the table while I get breakfast ready."

"I can't button," Jesse said, not moving toward the table but pointing to his unbuttoned shirt.

"That's going to have to wait for your mother. She should be done collecting eggs any moment."

"Please help, Grandma," Jesse said, as if he was trying the name on for size. Mrs. Whitaker sighed loudly, but she put down the spoon she was stirring the eggs with and buttoned Jesse's shirt.

"Now go sit at the table like I told you."

"Thank you, Grandma!"

"I asked you not to call me that."

Jesse climbed into one of the chairs at the table. "All right," he said, but Kate had a feeling he was going to call her whatever he wanted. Good for Jesse!

She walked into the house then, setting the egg basket on the counter. "Could I set the table for you?" she asked.

Mrs. Whitaker glared at her, but said nothing, so Kate went ahead and set the table, before pouring a glass of milk for Jesse. "I love all the colors of eggs your chickens lay. We only ever got brown and white."

"It's the breed of chickens. I had my husband get me a breed that would lay prettier eggs."

"Oh, how wonderful. I didn't know that."

"The Araucanas is my favorite breed. They're the ones who lay the plum-colored eggs you gathered this morning."

Kate looked down into the basket and smiled. "Those are my favorite eggs as well. I think you would look beautiful in that shade of purple."

Mrs. Whitaker glared at her. "How dare you suggest another color for me to wear while I'm in mourning! My husband just died last week, and I'll wear no color but black for a good long while yet."

Forcing her smile back to her face, Kate nodded. "Yes, ma'am. I won't suggest it again." But knowing that her mother-in-law liked the egg color, she could easily guess her favorite color. Maybe she wouldn't wear something pretty and new, but she could make some curtains in that shade for the parlor. It wouldn't exactly be a labor of love, more like an olive branch meant to help with the friction between the two of them.

Emmett came in a moment later, looking between them, as if he expected to see weapons somewhere. Kate smiled sweetly at him.

He said nothing as he put the pail of milk on the counter. His family had only ever kept enough cows to keep enough milk for them. The rest of the herd were for breeding.

When they were all sitting at the table together, Jesse asked, "I bet your eggs are the best I've ever tasted, Grandma!"

Mrs. Whitaker glared at him. "What are you supposed to call me?"

"My mouth doesn't like saying that name. It likes saying Grandma."

Emmett and Kate both watched the two of them, not hiding their interest in the conversation.

Mrs. Whitaker glared at both of them. "I should have known someone like you wouldn't be able to raise a child to have any manners."

Kate smiled and nodded. "Maybe you can help me with that. I've certainly done my best."

Emmett smiled. "I think he just wants to call you Grandma, Ma. Surely you can let a little boy call you by a name he likes."

"I will do no such thing!" Mrs. Whitaker said, shaking her head. "You're all three a bunch of loons."

Kate shrugged. "We probably are. Thank you for pointing that out."

There was a lull in the conversation for a moment. "What are you planning for today?" Kate asked Emmett.

"It's almost time to start branding the new calves. I know my father had a date in mind when he was going to invite all the neighbors for a branding party, but I don't think he's invited anyone yet. I believe we'll stick to that schedule. So, my chore today, will be starting to move them all into a pen so it will be easier once we have the necessary help here."

"Do you want me to address the invitations?" Kate asked. She knew there would need to be many people for the branding because she'd been part of it every year when her father had people come for the same purpose.

Mrs. Whitaker gasped, speaking as if she was offended. "That's one of my tasks! I've done it since before Emmett was born. You are not taking on my role in this house!"

Kate once again plastered a smile on her face. "I can work then. I have dresses to finish, and even one that needs to be delivered today." She looked at Emmett. "Perhaps you could hitch the wagon for me, and Jesse and I will ride into town. I may go ahead and turn my old place into a dress shop. It would be nice to have a place in town to work out of."

Emmett nodded. "Happy to do it." Of course, he understood that her main purpose in working in town would be to avoid his mother. She certainly was making life harder for everyone.

Jesse looked between his mother and Mrs. Whitaker. "Can I stay here with Grandma?" he asked.

Kate looked down and bit her lip to keep from laughing outright. As much as Mrs. Whitaker was determined to look down on Jesse, he was just as determined for her to like him.

"I don't think that's a good idea," Kate finally said. "You can nap in your old room while I work on getting a dress done for Aunt Florence. Her belly is getting big with her baby, isn't it?"

Jesse giggled. "It is. I almost couldn't fit on her lap."

Emmett smiled, liking the banter between mother and son. "Today's Friday, so we're going to Aunt Florence's house after church on Sunday. Won't that be fun?"

Mrs. Whitaker narrowed her eyes at Kate. "You only agreed to go there because you knew they don't allow me in their home."

Kate shook her head. "No, I had no idea. Why not?"

"Because Mr. Weatherby believes I should write a letter of apology to Mr. Weatherby about gossiping. I never gossip, so I wouldn't dream of writing a letter apologizing for what I didn't do. The last time they wanted to entertain my husband and me, he was the only one invited."

Kate's eyes widened. She hadn't known that a letter of apology had been requested, but she did know it had been Mrs. Whitaker's gossip which had made Florence aware of the situation she had with Jesse, and she had almost split up their marriage. "I suppose that's your choice, isn't it?" There was nothing else to say. The woman wouldn't even admit to being a gossip monger.

"Sorry, Mother. We've already accepted the invitation. Perhaps you could have a friend or two over for Sunday dinner here? We won't be taking up space."

Mrs. Whitaker said nothing, but her eyes narrowed at Kate. Obviously, it was Kate's fault she wasn't allowed in the nicest home in Cheyenne. Though, Kate wasn't sure how she'd managed such a thing.

Jesse hitched the wagon before heading out to work on his gelding. As soon as she'd finished the breakfast dishes—apparently she was good enough to wash dishes, just not good enough to cook—Kate and Jesse went to the wagon and put Kate's fabric and other business supplies into the wagon.

When she lifted Jesse onto the wagon seat, he frowned at her. "Mama, I want to stay with Grandma."

"Not yet, sweetie. Grandma needs to get to know you first. She just met you yesterday." Kate had no idea what excuse she'd come up with for not leaving her son with her mother-in-law the following day, but she knew that Jesse would not be staying with the woman who hated her so.

They both settled themselves into the old house, thankful that it was furnished. There was no need to do anything but empty the wagon and get to work. Jesse played on the floor while she worked, but he complained that he didn't have his wooden train there.

It was shortly before lunchtime when she realized that she'd forgotten to consider food. There was none in the house, so instead of spending the money eating out, Kate and Jesse walked over to Jake and Florence's residence on the other side of town. It wasn't a terribly long walk, and Kate was happy for the fresh air.

When Florence came to the door, Kate smiled. "Is it begging if I ask you to feed us because I forgot to bring any money with me for food when I ran away from the ranch this morning?"

Florence frowned. "You left Emmett?"

"No, of course not. I left his mother home alone for the day. Jesse and I had work to do."

"She doesn't like me to call her Grandma, but I like it so that's what I call her," Jesse said.

Florence looked like she wanted to laugh as hard as Kate had wanted to laugh that morning. "Jesse really likes Mrs. Whitaker."

"I've forgotten my manners," Florence said. "Come in and I'll let Mrs. Andrews know we'll need two more plates at the table." But she was too late. Jesse had already taken off toward the kitchen.

"Mrs. Andrews, I'm here!"

Kate shook her head, laughing. "That boy has got a mind of his own."

"Don't worry about it," Florence said. "Mrs. Andrews would rather spend time with Jesse than anyone else."

Sure enough, a smiling Mrs. Andrews came from the kitchen, carrying Jesse. "Are you staying for lunch as well, Miss Kate?"

Kate nodded. "I am, if you have enough."

Mrs. Andrews laughed. "Have you ever known me not to have enough?"

Kate enjoyed lunch with Florence. "I promise not to make a daily habit of this," she said halfway through the meal. "I wasn't about to sit at the ranch and let that woman be rude to me, so I came to town. I think I'm going to turn my little house into a dress shop. Then I'll have an excuse to leave every day."

Chapter Five

Kate did her best to time things so she would arrive home after Emmett was finished with work for the day. Unfortunately, she walked in the door and Emmett was nowhere to be seen. She held Jesse's hand as she walked into the kitchen. "Is there anything I can do to help?"

"You could have been here earlier to help with the cleaning!"

"I was under the impression you'd rather I wasn't here, so I spent the day in town. I'm going to turn my old house into a dress shop."

"I see. So, you won't be helping around the house at all then?"

"I'm happy to help in the evenings and on Sundays. If you'll make me a list of what I need to do, I could even get it done before work."

Mrs. Whitaker frowned. "I don't know why my son thought marrying you was a good idea."

"I don't either," Kate said honestly. "I don't deserve him, but I'm grateful he chose me."

Jesse let go of her hand and ran at Mrs. Whitaker. "I missed you, Grandma."

The look on Mrs. Whitaker's face had Kate trying her best not to laugh. She seemed to be torn between returning Jesse's hug and pushing him away. In the end, she patted his back.

Kate held her hand out for Jesse. "Let's go upstairs, and you can play in your room."

Jesse looked up at Mrs. Whitaker. "I want to stay with Grandma."

"It's probably better if you spend some time with me."

Mrs. Whitaker took a deep breath. "He can stay down here with me. I'm baking cookies, and I'll need someone to taste them and make certain they're good."

Kate nodded. "All right. Is there a chore or two I could accomplish while he's down here with you then?"

"Yes, there is. I need someone to clean the bathroom. Make sure you scrub the toilet."

Smiling sweetly, Kate nodded. "I'd be happy to." She knew it wasn't the reaction her mother-in-law wanted, but she was determined not to let the woman get her down. Emmett was a wonderful husband so far, and Kate wasn't about to make his life harder by arguing with his mother.

Once she was done in the bathroom, Kate returned to the kitchen, listening for a moment in the dining room where she could hear, but not be seen. "I think you should make the cookies bigger, Grandma!"

"This is a good size for a cookie."

"Will you make a bigger one just for me?" Jesse asked.

There was a loud sigh. "You're determined to make me like you, aren't you, boy?"

Jesse giggled. "I love you, Grandma!"

Kate chose that moment to make her presence known. "I finished the bathroom. Is there anything else I can do to help?"

Mrs. Whitaker was still frowning at Jesse. "I will plant the kitchen garden starting on Monday. Perhaps Jesse could help me."

"I think he'd like that a lot," Kate said. She wasn't certain what it was about Mrs. Whitaker that Jesse was so drawn to, but she wasn't going to complain.

"Oh, yes! I will be the best garden helper ever!"

Mrs. Whitaker looked at Kate. "He's a bright boy."

Kate smiled. "I'm pretty proud of him."

"You can set the table," Mrs. Whitaker said. "I guess I don't have to do all of the cooking and serving."

"I'd be happy to."

While Jesse stayed in the kitchen, Kate set the table. She wished Emmett would hurry and return home, but Mrs. Whitaker was being downright pleasant—for her.

When Kate heard the front door open, she smiled. That had to be Emmett.

Emmett walked inside. "I'm home!"

Kate hurried to him. "Did you have a good day?" He was covered in dirt, and she could smell the sweat on him.

He nodded. "Yes, very much so. There are three times more calves than I expected. When we take them to market in the spring, we're going to make a pretty penny." He leaned down and kissed her. "How was your day?"

"It was good. I finished another dress, and Jesse and I delivered it. I've let some people know that my old house will be my dress shop, and they said they would spread the news."

"Wonderful. It will be nice if you can have people pick up from your store instead of having to deliver everything."

Kate nodded. "There are still some people I'll go to their home to help, but for the most part, they can come to me. I'm even considering making dresses so people can buy them as they are to build up an inventory. Of course, I have to catch up on my current orders first."

"Is that going to take long?" he asked.

"Depends on how many orders I get before I'm done. I'm thinking about buying a sewing machine, which would speed everything up a great deal, but would take most of the money I have saved."

"I think you should do it," he said. "You'll be able to do your work in a fraction of the time, and you'll make up for the cost with faster service."

"Do you really think so?" she asked. It was something she'd been contemplating for a long time.

"I really do."

Mrs. Whitaker stuck her head out of the kitchen. "Supper's ready. Kate, I'd appreciate it if you'd help me put the food on the table."

Kate nodded and immediately went to help. As Emmett watched, he realized that things seemed to be going better between his wife and his mother, which thrilled him. Perhaps Kate just needed to be herself and his mother would realize how much she was missing out on by not knowing her.

Once supper was on the table, Emmett prayed over the meal, and then they started fixing their plates. Kate cut up Jesse's meat and put his plate in front of him. "I wanted Grandma to cut up my meat," Jesse said, pushing his plate away.

Kate looked at Emmett, wondering how to respond. To her surprise, Mrs. Whitaker took Jesse's plate and made the pieces even smaller. "How's that?" she asked.

Jesse smiled. "Thank you, Grandma."

Emmett seemed more than a little curious about what had brought that about, but Kate shook her head, silently begging him to say nothing. "Are you going into town to work tomorrow?" he asked Kate.

"I thought I'd just be open from Monday through Friday. I can stay here tomorrow and help out around the house. The flower garden out front looks like it needs a good weeding. I miss getting my hands covered in dirt as I did."

Emmett smiled. "I think that's a great idea."

"Your mother and Jesse will be planting the kitchen garden on Monday. You may want to have someone plow the land she's going to use."

Mrs. Whitaker nodded. "I need a large plot. There are four of us this year, and we'll need more food to make it through the year."

Emmett nodded. "I'm happy to have someone help."

After supper, Kate did the dishes while Emmett bathed, and Jesse spent his time in the parlor with his new grandmother. Just as she finished the dishes, Emmett popped his head into the kitchen. "I was thinking a walk would be nice this evening."

Kate nodded. "That sounds lovely. Let's see if Jesse wants to go. I don't want your mother to think I only want her to mind my child."

Emmett nodded, planning to ask many questions about what was happening. In the parlor, he asked Jesse, "Do you want to walk with me and your mama?" he asked.

Jesse looked from his new father to Mrs. Whitaker. "Can I stay with you, Grandma?"

Mrs. Whitaker nodded. "Sure. We need to try those cookies we made, don't we?"

Jesse nodded. "With milk!"

"I like milk with my cookies too."

Emmett looked at Kate. "I guess it's just the two of us."

"Guess so."

As soon as they were far enough away from the house not to be heard, Emmett asked, "What happened between Jesse and Mother today?"

Kate shrugged. "I honestly have no idea. Jesse refused to call her Mrs. Whitaker. Then he asked to stay with her all day while I worked, but I said no. When I got home, she scolded me for not helping clean, but then I offered to do whatever she wanted. Next thing I knew, those two were fast friends."

"Do you trust her with him?" he asked.

"I really don't know. I mean, I want them to be close, because the more time she spends with him, the kinder she is to me."

"Which makes sense, I think..."

"I'm just glad she's not being unkind to him. He ran at her and embraced her when we returned this afternoon, and though she didn't hug him, she did pat his back. I guess they've decided to be grandmother and grandson."

Emmett smiled. "I'm just glad she wasn't as mean to you today as she was yesterday. Maybe she's truly understanding that you're my wife, and nothing is going to change that."

"Maybe?" It didn't make sense to Kate, but she would go along with just about anything as long as Mrs. Whitaker wasn't cruel to her son. "It sounds like you had a good day at work."

He nodded. "I haven't ridden much since leaving almost five years ago, so my bottom is a bit sore, but other than that, I'm good."

"Glad to hear it. Any trouble with the men?"

"Not at all. The man who was Pa's foreman when I left still is. So there was no problem getting the men to follow my orders. Bob made sure everything was still all right after Pa died, and he was just waiting for me to return so I could take over. Everyone else followed his example."

"That's great. When are we doing the branding party?"

"Two weeks from Friday, and it will go through Saturday. Lots of work to do."

"It sounds like it. I'm just glad everything is running smoothly, and the transition is easy."

He nodded. "I am as well. Sounds like Pa said good things about me to the men, and that made things easier as well. I really expected to have to show my ability to lead them, but that hasn't been the case at all."

"So the only struggle for power around here is the one in the house between your mother and me. I'm letting your mother win that one, though. There's no need for me to fight her. I have a business to run, and I'm happy to let her do the cooking and housework. I'll help where needed, but if she doesn't trust me to do things, then I can just get out of the house and go work."

"That works for me. I don't need you to be the one cooking my meals or making the bed..."

"Oh, I make sure our bed and Jesse's are made when I get up. I'm not going to have her calling me lazy and have to agree, even in my own mind."

He chuckled. "Sounds like you're doing everything you should be doing then."

"I am," she said. "I do think she's softening toward me. I know she's softening toward Jesse."

"I was really surprised by how he was with her this evening. It's hard to believe there's been such a change since I left for work this morning."

"I know! I think it helps that I'm not underfoot all day though. I can go to town and work, and she can forget I exist for a few hours. And she asked for Jesse to stay home with her on Monday so he could help her with the planting. Jesse's very excited at the prospect."

"I guess miracles do happen." He shook his head. "I should have brought my camera!"

"Why is that?" she asked. "Oh for the sunset?" The sky was gorgeous that night, and she would have loved if they could have had a photograph of it.

"No, because I'd love to capture your photo in this light. You're always beautiful, but with the sun behind you, you're stunning."

Kate shook her head, laughing. "You don't have to say things like that to me just because we're married. I know what I look like. I have a mirror."

"You really think I'm just saying that? Do you not know me at all?" His feelings were a bit hurt when she didn't believe him.

"I don't know you well," she answered softly. "I haven't seen you for five years, and then it was only at school."

"I suppose that's true. I guess we'll have to spend some time exploring one another tonight."

She caught his meaning and laughed. "You only think of one thing!"

He grinned. "I guess I love being married to a special woman. Is that so difficult to believe?" He stopped walking and pulled her to him by the hand he was holding. "I don't think I've kissed you in front of a sunset before."

"I don't think you have! And you call yourself a husband!"

"I call myself your husband." He lowered his head to hers and kissed her until her toes were curling inside her shoes. "What do you think the chances of us getting caught making love out here are?"

"Too strong to risk it!" she responded. As much as she enjoyed his lovemaking, the idea of being stumbled on made it impossible for her.

He sighed. "I guess we should go home then. Do you think Ma would notice if we didn't talk to her and went straight upstairs so we could enjoy one another?"

She shook her head. "We're not doing that. She already thinks I'm lazy. I can just hear her at the next society dinner. 'That daughter-in-law of mine is a lazy whore. She spends all her time trying to entice my perfect son into her bed. I think you'll all agree that needs to stop. Oh, woah is me.'"

Emmett laughed. "Wonderful impression of her. But if she calls you a whore again, and you hear about it, I want you to tell me."

"I will," she promised.

Emmett started walking back toward the house. "Do you think any of those cookies are left? Or did Jesse and Ma polish them all off."

"I hope there are some left," she said. "Cookies and milk sound wonderful right now."

"Then we'd better hurry so we can be certain we'll have some!" He sped up walking. "If I wasn't so sore from riding all day, I'd challenge you to a race."

She giggled. "Then imagine what your mother would say."

Chapter Six

Saturday went much better than expected for Kate. She spent a good deal of time weeding the flowers in the front of the house, with Jesse "helping."

When it was time for lunch, Mrs. Whitaker called them in, and they had a pleasant lunch. Jesse asked if he could stay inside after lunch, and when Kate told him he needed to take a nap, Mrs. Whitaker offered to listen for him.

"Thank you. That would help a great deal. Is there anything else I can help you with today? I'm almost done with the flower garden out front."

Mrs. Whitaker shook her head. "No, just the flower garden. Unless you want to clean the chicken coop. It's been needing it for a while."

Kate nodded. "I can do that." She hated cleaning chicken coops. They always smelled and cleaning them was a very dirty job. But she wasn't about to refuse to do the dirty jobs around the house. She wished she was allowed to cook a little, but Mrs. Whitaker seemed to enjoy it.

"Thank you," Mrs. Whitaker said, seeming to genuinely mean it. How odd.

As soon as she'd done the dishes, which seemed to be her permanent task in the household, Kate went out to work on the chicken coop. It took her hours, but when she was done, she was pleased with the result.

When she went back into the house, she hurried upstairs to get some clean clothes and went into the bathroom to clean herself up. After a long bath, she was ready to face clean people again.

Emmett came in for the day just as she was leaving the bathroom. "Do you want a bath before supper?" she asked.

At his nod, she offered to bring him clothes downstairs, so he could get right in. "I'd love that." He looked exhausted after his long day of work, and she didn't blame him. She was certain she hadn't worked nearly as hard as he had, and she was exhausted as well. There was something about working outside that tired her out much faster than working in the house.

She hurried up the stairs and got him some clean clothes from the dresser, taking them back down. She carried them into the bathroom and set them down. "Clothes are here," she called before leaving the bathroom to see if Mrs. Whitaker needed help with supper.

"What can I do to help?" Kate asked. She'd determined that it was easier if she asked what she could do instead of asking if there was anything. She was more likely to be given tasks that way.

Jesse was standing on a chair that was faced backward and he was dredging chicken in flour. As she watched, he dipped it in the egg wash and then dipped it into the flour before placing it on a plate that Mrs. Whitaker was taking chicken from and frying. "It looks like you have lots of help!"

"I'm a good helper," Jesse said, turning around to look at his mother. The front of his hair, all of his face, and his shirt were completely covered in flour.

"I can see that," Kate said, grinning at his appearance. "I think I need to plan to do laundry before church tomorrow."

Jesse shrugged. "That's okay. I'll play with Grandma."

"How can I help?" Kate asked again.

"Set the table, and if you can mash the potatoes, I'd be grateful." Mrs. Whitaker didn't bother to look at her, but her tone was certainly sweeter than Kate was used to.

Kate set the table first, and then she took the pot of potatoes off the stove and carefully drained them. She added milk, butter, salt, and pepper and mashed the potatoes quickly, a task she'd been performing for a long time. When that was done, she poured the potatoes into a bowl, so they were ready to serve.

"Anything else?"

"Put some butter and that loaf of bread on the table," Mrs. Whitaker said, nodding to the bread she'd baked that day.

After Jesse had finished his task, Kate cleaned him up as best she could with a pitcher of water. "You're taking a bath after supper," she told him.

"Why?" Jesse asked, making faces as she scrubbed his face.

"Because you have so much flour on you, if I shook you off, we'd have enough for another loaf of bread!"

"That's cuz I was helping," he told her.

Kate smiled. "You did a good job helping."

Emmett walked out of the bathroom then, smelling much better than he had going in. "What did you help with?" he asked Jesse, picking the boy up and setting him on his shoulder.

Jesse giggled. "I helped Grandma fry the chicken! I dipped it in egg and got flour all over it, and then she put it in the pan. I was a good helper!"

"It sounds like it!" Emmett said. "I guess if it doesn't taste good, I should blame you."

"No!" Jesse said. "Blame Mama."

"I wasn't involved with frying the chicken!" she said. "Why would you blame me?"

"We can't blame Grandma," Jesse said. "She worked hard to cook supper."

"I guess we just can't blame anyone then," Kate said.

"Kate!" Mrs. Whitaker called from the kitchen. Kate hurried to see what she could do to help. "Will you put the gravy on, while I bring in the chicken? You're going to have a big mess to clean after supper."

Kate smiled. "I've already been working on my big mess of a son, but I'm happy to clean in here as well."

"I don't think I've ever seen a child wear that much flour!" Mrs. Whitaker said, shaking her head as she put the chicken onto the table. "I will give him a bath after supper while you do the dishes and get the kitchen cleaned."

"Sounds good." Kate was truly surprised at how easily she and Mrs. Whitaker were working together to get all the chores accomplished.

Emmett smiled as he sat down at the head of the table, obviously pleased at how well the two of them were getting on after a very rocky start.

While they ate, Mrs. Whitaker addressed Kate. "I have a banquet I need to go to for the hospital next month. Do you think you could make me a dress for it?"

"Of course. I can show you my sketches after supper tonight."

"Your sketches?"

"Yes, all the dresses I make are my own designs, and I make little changes to each dress, so no two ladies in town are wearing the same dress," Kate said.

"What kind of changes?" Mrs. Whitaker asked.

"If two people love the same design, I'll talk one of them into letting me embroider flowers on the collar. Or I'll add different sleeves or let them choose a different neckline. It's fun for me to come up with ways for the dresses to be different."

"I'll look forward to seeing your sketches then."

Once the kitchen was finally clean, Kate went upstairs to fetch her design book to show her mother-in-law. A lot of work had gone into the designs, and she was excited to show her. She already had a dress in mind for her, and she would try to talk her into the style, but there was no telling how Mrs. Whitaker would react to anything. She'd been surprised more often than not that week.

Taking the book into the parlor, she laid it across her lap and Mrs. Whitaker's where they sat on the sofa. As she flipped through the pages, Mrs. Whitaker liked a few of the designs. When she landed on the design she thought the woman should have, Kate paused. "This is the one I like best for you," she said softly. "I'd raise the neckline for you a little, because I think it would look better on you that way. And I wouldn't keep the sleeves this puffy. I'd make them more fitted, and take them down to your wrists."

Mrs. Whitaker stared at the dress, imagining what Kate was saying and nodding. "I agree. What color do you think I should do?"

Kate smiled. "I think we should do the plum color of the eggs you like so much."

"Oh, I don't know about that…"

"Unless you still want to wear your mourning colors, and I could make it in black." Kate said a silent prayer her mother-in-law would agree to the plum color they both liked. It would look so much better on her than black, and by then it would be six weeks of mourning. That was longer than most women mourned in the west.

"All right," Mrs. Whitaker said. "Make it in the plum."

Kate smiled. "I'll get your measurements before I go to town on Monday."

"How much will this dress cost?"

"This is a gift. You're family."

Mrs. Whitaker seemed genuinely shocked. "I know this is how you make your living…"

"It was. Now it's extra money for doing something I enjoy a great deal."

"All right."

KATE WOKE AT DAWN THE following morning to get the laundry done before church. It would dry while they were gone, and she could take it in from the line after they had lunch at the Weatherbys'.

She gathered all the laundry she found in the basket outside the bathroom and carried it outside. She'd happily do her mother-in-law's laundry along with hers, Emmett's, and Jesse's. It was easier to do it all at once anyway.

By the time the house was waking, she had finished hanging the laundry on the line and gathered eggs. The chicken coop certainly smelled much better than it had the day before, and as much as Kate hated it at the time, she was glad she'd done it.

When she took the eggs inside, Mrs. Whitaker seemed less friendly than she had, but Kate decided not to ask. She couldn't imagine she'd done anything wrong between the evening before and now, so she simply stayed out of the woman's way.

She got Jesse up and put him in his play clothes. She'd change him again before church, but she didn't want to risk him wearing his breakfast to church. She even packed a bag of clean clothes for him for after church when they would eat at Florence's house. It was easier to change him than clean his nice church clothes.

She took him downstairs and set the table without being asked. Jesse stood beside his grandmother and asked what they were having for breakfast.

"I'm making flapjacks," she said, but her voice wasn't as kind as it had been the night before. "I don't want you to call me Grandma at church."

"But I can call you Grandma at home?" he asked.

At her nod, he shrugged. "All right, Grandma."

Suddenly Kate understood. She'd been the object of the woman's gossip for long enough that she couldn't imagine how embarrassing it would be for Mrs. Whitaker if Jesse called her Grandma at church.

"I'll do my best to keep him away from you at church, so he doesn't accidentally slip up," Kate said.

Mrs. Whitaker's eyes were wide, as if she hadn't expected Kate to understand her problem with Jesse calling her Grandma. "Thank you," she said, still looking a bit embarrassed.

Kate smiled, but this time her smile wasn't as bright. It had never occurred to her the older woman would be so embarrassed to have her and Jesse as part of her family. She wanted to say something rude, but what difference would it make? Mrs. Whitaker was the worst gossip in town, and she was afraid all of her friends would turn on her over her son's choices.

After breakfast, Kate took Jesse back upstairs to dress him in his Sunday best, and she was aware that Emmett had followed her. "What happened between you and mother this morning?"

"Nothing really. She's afraid Jesse will call her Grandma at church, and everyone will know that you married me. That's the real issue. Nothing has happened yet, but she's afraid that it will." He looked angry, and she shook her head. "Don't worry about it. It's just how she is, and I knew it when I married you. I just thought that things were getting easier between us, and things would be better going forward. I guess I hadn't considered that Jesse calling her Grandma would be such a big deal."

Emmett was already in his Sunday best, so he went down the stairs and confronted his mother. "You love that little boy, and I can see you really enjoy it when he calls you Grandma, but you are afraid other people will know about it if he does it at church?" he asked.

Ma just shrugged. "Our family name doesn't need to be colored that way."

"I'm married to Kate, and that's not changing. I love her, Ma, and I need you to start working to get along with her."

"I have been! I let her boy call me Grandma. I let her help around the house. I haven't been mean to her. This is hard for me!"

"Maybe it's time for me to get that cabin ready for you. I don't think you should be treating my wife like she's not good enough to be married to me simply because she's had a baby."

"You don't understand the scandal she caused when it came out she was pregnant. And the fact that Jacob Weatherby wouldn't even marry her? Her own parents had to leave town."

"Jesse Weatherby is Jesse's father. Not Jake. He died the day before they were to be married, and Kate was expecting. She hadn't realized there would be a scandal. How could she? She was about to marry the man!"

Ma shook her head. "It's not a good enough reason. She never should have laid with a man she wasn't married to. It's that simple. And her son just rubs it in everyone's face that she was a woman of loose morals."

"She may not be perfect in your eyes, but she's perfect in mine. You need to get along with her, and you need to treat her, and our son well."

"He's not your son!"

"He is now. I married his mother, and her son is now mine as well as hers. I would thank you to remember that in future." He put his hat on his head. "I'm going out to hitch up both buggies. You'll drive yourself to church and back because we're still having lunch with the Weatherbys."

"Now won't that just add to the gossip?" she asked.

"I really don't care if it does. But I will care if you add to the gossip."

He stomped out toward the stable, furious with his mother. How could she insult his wife and the boy who loved her so much he refused not to call her Grandma? She needed to learn that everyone in the world didn't judge people the way she did.

Chapter Seven

Church that morning was different than Emmett had ever experienced. Kate wanted to sit in the back right corner of the church, where she'd been sitting since before Jesse was born. "People don't notice me back here, and there's less gossip."

He shook his head. "Now that we're married, there's bound to be more gossip than ever. We'll sit where we want, and let people choke on their judgment."

"I promised your mother, I'd keep Jesse away from her."

"Come on." He led her to the front of the church, and they took a pew off to the right. He wasn't surprised to see Florence and Jake move to sit with them.

"Safety in numbers," Jake whispered as he proudly sat between his wife and Jesse.

Jesse looked just like his uncle, which made sense because his father was Jake's identical twin.

As always, many people came to talk to Florence, but no one even acknowledged Kate. Finally, Florence had enough. The next woman who walked over to talk to her, she smiled and introduced Kate. "Oh, I know Kate. She made me this dress," the woman said.

"And her husband is Mrs. Whitaker's son, Emmett. Do you know Emmett?"

The woman's jaw dropped. "Emmett Whitaker married Kate Jessup?"

Emmett stood. "I did. She's a wonderful wife. I'm very proud of her."

The woman stood for a moment. "I...see. Excuse me!" Without another word, she scurried off to where Julie Whitaker was sitting across the church. Kate had no idea what was said, but whatever it was, Mrs. Whitaker was glaring at her yet again.

"Now you've done it," Kate said softly.

"Done what?" Florence asked. "Made a bunch of hypocritical women acknowledge your existence?"

"Mrs. Whitaker and I have actually been getting along quite well. Jesse has fallen in love with her and calls her Grandma, though she did ask him not to call her that in church."

"So she can talk to you when you're not in public, but as soon as you're in front of other people, you're not good enough. Is that what you're saying?" Florence looked angry enough to march across the church and give the women a piece of her mind, and there was no doubt in Kate's mind she'd actually do it. It had happened once before, and things had actually changed.

Kate put her hand on Florence's arm. "I'm handling things in my own way."

"I don't like to see you mistreated," Florence said. "She makes me so mad I could just spit!"

At that, Kate couldn't hold back a giggle. Florence was every inch a lady, and the idea of her spitting on someone was outrageous. "You're not spitting on her or anyone else," Kate told her friend.

Jesse sat beside Kate, holding her hand. "I'm going to go tell Grandma I love her. She looks sad."

"That's not a very good idea right now," Kate said, afraid of how the older woman would treat Jesse if he went to her at church.

Thankfully, the pastor was in front of them all, inviting them to sing a hymn. After the hymn, the pastor started his sermon, surprising Kate with his frank talk. "I want to address a topic that I think is turning our community into an unwholesome place where none of us will be happy to live. Let me ask all of you if there is one person in this church who has never sinned. Do you gossip? That's a huge sin. Do you commit adultery? Do you envy? Do you covet? All of those things are sins. Jesus never gave us a level of sins. He died for every person's sins, not just for the sin you're thinking of, but all of them. Judging your fellow man is a sin. I know many of you have been judgmental of others. I see a sweet young woman who recently got married. She had a child before she married, but now she's a wife and a mother. Should we continue to judge her simply because she was caught in her sin? I don't think so."

The entire sermon was about judging others, and as much as the entire congregation needed the sermon, Kate hated that she'd been mentioned. Oh, not everyone would know it had been her the preacher talked about, but enough would. She was greatly saddened by the lack of compassion she'd received, but there shouldn't be a sermon about it, should there?

After church, Kate couldn't make eye contact with anyone. Oh, she and Florence were fine, and she and Jake were fine, but she didn't feel like she should make contact even with Emmett. He had to be terribly embarrassed that she'd been part of the sermon. She wanted to run, but she had to teach Jesse not to run from his fears, and she wouldn't run from that.

Emmett offered her his arm, and he had a look of pride on his face. She took his arm, while wishing the floor would open up and swallow her whole.

As they left the church, she noticed that no one was making eye contact with her either. They'd all recognized that it was her the pastor was talking about, so of course, they'd avoid her.

As soon as she was in the buggy heading toward Florence's house, she whispered, "I'm so sorry!"

Emmett seemed genuinely confused. "About what?"

"That our first church service as a married couple was about me and my sins."

He frowned at her. "You didn't listen very well, did you?"

"I have no idea what you mean by that."

"The pastor was talking about how all of us sin. That the fact that you were caught in your sin, doesn't make it any worse than the sins the rest of us commit. And he was talking about the gossip and judgment that the women in town are full of. Oh, probably the men as well, but the women are the ones who gossip about you, not the men."

"But he stood there and talked about how I had a child before marriage! He singled me out to talk about my sin."

"No, that's not what happened. He was trying to tell the whole congregation to stop talking about you. He wants them to treat you the way they treat everyone else. Their sins are just as bad as yours, and you have no reason to hang your head in shame. Your sin was years ago. Their sins have been going on for years. Who do you think is more sinful in God's eyes? The one who committed a sin and has paid for it every day of her life since? Or the people who talked badly about her every day since?"

She frowned. "I don't know..."

"I do." He pulled the buggy to a stop in front of the Weatherbys' house. "Are you still up for Sunday dinner with them? Or would you rather go home?"

"No, let's eat with them. I don't think I could face your mother right now."

"I don't think she could face you," he said.

She shook her head but let him help her down from the buggy and they went into the house. Florence was excited. "I loved the sermon! Oh, all those harridans will be put in their place by that. Well, those that bothered to listen anyway."

Kate looked between Emmett and Florence. "Were you two at a different service than I was?"

Florence laughed. "You just didn't pay attention. I think as soon as he mentioned the word sin, you blocked everything else out. He was saying all of our sins were exactly the same. And that means yours is the same as those evil people gossiping about you. I'm so ready not to hear gossip about you. It's been almost five years!"

Kate nodded, moving into the house. Jake walked to her and hugged her close, as he always did when they were private. "Hello, little sister."

Kate smiled. "Hello! Do you know Emmett?"

Jake shook his head. "I've heard of him, of course." He stuck out a hand to shake Emmett's. "So good to meet you. You married a wonderful woman."

Emmett smiled. "I agree. She puts a smile on my face every day."

As they sat down to lunch, Jesse ran into the kitchen to be with Mrs. Andrews. Emmett frowned. "Jesse isn't eating with us?"

Florence laughed. "Jesse is with Mrs. Andrews, who he thinks of as his grandmother. She eats with him and spoils him rotten."

Kate raised an eyebrow at her friend. "She didn't buy him all those toys when he was here earlier in the week."

Florence shrugged. "I didn't get him anything he didn't like."

Jake shook his head. "I'm glad to see you back in town," he said to Emmett. "I know you were in Kate's class at school, right?"

"Yes," Emmett said. "She was always one of my favorite people. When it was her I ended up marrying instead of someone else, I must say I was pleased. I thought she'd married your brother."

"She was supposed to. I even asked her to marry me, but she said no. I guess I don't hold a candle to you or Jesse."

Kate glared at him. "You asked me to marry you so I wouldn't be pregnant and alone. Don't try to make it sound like you were in love with me."

Jake grinned. "I don't know why you would think that!"

Florence rolled her eyes. "Behave yourself, Jake. Emmett will believe you, and then where will you be?"

Jake laughed. "All right. I asked her to marry me because my brother was dead, and she was carrying his child."

"The next time she carries a child, she's not going to be alone," Emmett said softly.

"How is your mother handling your marriage?" Jake asked, imagining the worst.

"She wasn't happy at first, and she still says she isn't now, but I think she likes having Kate there to help with chores, and Jesse calls her Grandma, and I have to say, I think she's fallen in love with him. They spend a lot of time together."

Kate nodded. "It surprised me a lot. All day yesterday, I was working on weeding flowers, and then I cleaned out the chicken coop. Jesse was inside with Mrs. Whitaker, and they had a wonderful day. When I went in after cleaning the coop, I found Jesse dipping chicken into an egg wash, and then into flour. He was cooking fried chicken with her!"

Florence laughed. "I can just imagine the mess."

Kate sighed. "It was awful. He was covered with flour. The kitchen was covered with flour. I swear I could have shaken the boy and had enough flour for a loaf of bread. And I got to clean the kitchen, but Mrs. Whitaker gave him a bath, and I heard laughter coming from the bathroom. Both of them were laughing, not just Jesse."

"That's amazing!" Florence said. "He needs a toy boat for something to play with in the bathtub."

"I agree," Kate said. "But I've never seen one at the mercantile."

"Let me handle the boat," Emmett said, a gleam in his eye.

Kate looked at her husband, but he was giving nothing away, so she turned back to Florence. "Mrs. Whitaker even ordered a dress from me. I think I'm going to buy a machine tomorrow."

"Oh really? Do you know how to use one?" Florence asked, looking excited.

"I've seen them, but I've never actually touched one. How difficult can it be to learn to use a machine whose sole purpose is to make women's jobs easier?"

"Hopefully, not difficult at all!" Florence said. "I'm excited you're getting it. I know you've wanted to for a while. What made you decide to actually do it?"

"I talked to Emmett about it. When my business was my sole income, it didn't make sense. But now that Emmett works to support our family, I can spare money I have saved to buy a machine to make more. I know I should simply quit working, but I enjoy what I do so much. And it's so nice not to have to worry about our income!"

"I'll worry for you," Emmett said.

"You're a good husband," Kate replied, smiling at him. All at once, she realized he really was exactly what she'd needed. She hadn't stopped to think about it before. He was good with Jesse, he was good with her, and she had no worries about finances. Who could ask for more from a man?

"I do my best."

On their way home later that afternoon, Kate thought again about how good he was for her. How on earth had she dismissed him when they were in school?

"What are your plans this week?" she asked.

He shrugged. "Working. I need to spend a day going over the ranch's numbers, but I'm still getting everyone used to me running the place. What about you?"

"I'm going to buy that sewing machine tomorrow, and I'll go into town to work as long as your mother doesn't need me. I think it's better for me to stay out of her way for the most part. I'm not exactly her favorite person."

"You need to stop worrying about my mother so much."

She sighed. "I'm in her house every day. She's just started letting me do the dishes and help around the house. I don't know how you expect me to stop worrying about her. What if she says something mean to Jesse and breaks his little heart?"

Jesse was sleeping in her arms. He hadn't been ready to wake up from his nap when it was time for them to head home.

"I don't think she will," Emmett said. "She loves Jesse. If you watch them together, I think you'll see that. She's not going to upset her biggest ally in the family. She knows I back you completely, and that you back me. Jesse is the only one who thinks she makes the sun rise and set."

"I guess..."

"Trust me. I hope she's different to you after today's sermon anyway. She sure should be."

"I hope she is too." But she wasn't going to hold her breath. Mrs. Whitaker had been against her for way too long for her to believe it was possible for her to change.

"It'll be better, or I'll have the cabin fixed up, and I'll move her to it myself. She may be my mother, but that doesn't give her the right to mistreat my wife. Ever. I probably should have moved her out already, but I wanted to give her a chance to get used to our marriage before I took that drastic of an action."

"I don't want your mother to have to move out of the only home she's known for the past twenty-five years."

"Neither do I. But if it comes down to a choice, it would have to be my wife." And the woman I love, he silently added. She wasn't ready for the words yet, but that didn't mean he couldn't think them.

Chapter Eight

Mrs. Whitaker was oddly quiet when Emmett, Kate, and Jesse arrived home that afternoon. Emmett carried Jesse up to his bed while Kate took the laundry off the line and ironed what needed to be ironed.

As soon as she was finished, she put away her clothes, as well as Emmett's and Jesse's. Then she went into the kitchen where Mrs. Whitaker was. "I finished the laundry. I put yours into a basket to be put away because I didn't want to go into your room without permission."

Mrs. Whitaker frowned. "Thank you."

"You're welcome. What can I do to help you?"

"Nothing to do. I have supper going, and we have fresh baked bread. We're all caught up on housework, which is something I thought I'd never be able to say."

Kate smiled. "It's nice to say it on a Sunday because then there's time for enjoying one's family. How would you feel if I made us a pot of tea? Emmett went up to nap at the same time Jesse did. He said he's not used to working a ranch all day."

"That would be nice."

Kate filled the kettle and set the table with teacups and small plates, planning on serving a few of the cookies Mrs. Whitaker and Jesse had made the previous day. As soon as the tea was ready, Kate served it and took the seat near Mrs. Whitaker's chair.

"We had a lovely time with the Weatherbys," Kate said, wanting to strike up a conversation. "Jake's housekeeper raised him after his parents died, so Jesse thinks of her as a grandmother. When we walk into the house, he starts shouting, 'I'm here!' so she'll come and spoil him."

"He's a very sweet boy. You've done a good job with him so far." Mrs. Whitaker hadn't met her gaze, and her voice was soft.

"He has a way with people, that's for certain."

"Who is Jesse's father?" Mrs. Whitaker asked. There was no accusation in her voice for once, and it was obviously a question driven by curiosity, and not something sinister.

"Jacob Weatherby had an identical twin brother. Jesse and I were engaged and anticipated our wedding vows by a week. He died the day before the wedding. Jake offered to marry me so there wouldn't be a scandal, but I didn't love Jake, and he didn't love me. So he's helped me out with finances from time to time, but I never thought it made sense to marry. I adore his new wife, Florence."

"So all those rumors about you and Jake..."

"They were false," Kate said. "I hated that Jake was painted with the same tar everyone painted me with, but he told me to keep smiling, and eventually, it would blow over."

Mrs. Whitaker shook her head. "I do owe him and his wife an apology then, don't I?"

Kate nodded. "The entire town does, in my opinion. When you told Florence about me, she was very upset. As soon as she knew the truth, she apologized to Jake, but damage had been done. It took them a while to sort through their feelings."

"But she was your first customer!"

"She was, and we've become close friends. She ordered an entire wardrobe when she'd just had one made. That way, she could talk around town about what a wonderful seamstress I was. She was the perfect model for my designs." Kate smiled. "My business never would have taken off if not for Florence."

"It would have been easier if people hadn't said things behind your back to begin with."

Kate shrugged. "Don't worry. Nothing said behind my back was ever not said to my face."

"Why did your parents leave?" Mrs. Whitaker asked.

"They were embarrassed by my loose morals. Of course, I've never really had loose morals. I intended to be a virgin when I married, but things just happened. I'm thankful I'm finished with that difficulty."

"I don't blame you," Mrs. Whitaker said. "I'm very sorry for how I've treated you, both before and after you married Emmett. That sermon today woke me up in a way that I shouldn't have needed."

Kate couldn't believe her ears. Mrs. Whitaker had actually apologized? Kate put her hand over her mother-in-law's. "I forgive you. I want us to get along so we can live together peacefully."

"I want that too," Mrs. Whitaker said with a tear in her eye. "I love Emmett's father, whom I always loved. Now I've been given a chance with you and Jesse to love the people Emmett loves. I just didn't want you for a daughter, and not because of Jesse. I remember how heartbroken Emmett was when you got engaged, and I don't want him to go through that again."

Kate frowned. "You must be thinking of someone else! Emmett and I were only friends when we were children. We were in the same grade at school."

Mrs. Whitaker frowned. "I must be mistaken then. I could have sworn it was you who broken his heart."

"I don't think it's possible to break a heart and have no knowledge of it," Kate said, munching on her cookie.

"I'm sure you're right," Mrs. Whitaker said. "You should go sit on the front porch and read or something. You work all the time."

Kate sipped the last of her tea. "I'll clean up the mess I've made, and then I'll go. I don't have any books, but I can just sit and think."

"I have novels you can borrow. They're all in the parlor. Pick any book you like!"

Kate smiled, loving the idea of sitting and reading for a while. It had been her favorite pastime as a child. "Thank you, Mrs. Whitaker. I'll take good care of your books."

"Please, call me Julie."

Not quite able to believe the conversation she'd just had with her mother-in-law, Kate smiled as she did the dishes and put them away. She chose a book from the shelf in the parlor and went out onto the front porch to read. What a blessing to have a time when there was nothing she had to be doing. A week before, she never would have guessed there would ever be that kind of time. Well, not until Jesse grew up at least.

She had over an hour to simply sit and read before Emmett joined her on the swing. She kept her voice as low as she could while she told him all that had transpired between his mother and her.

"Thank God for good sermons," he whispered back.

"That's my thought," she said. "I guess I was silly for blaming it all on myself."

"You were, but that's also a good quality. You hear something that could be improved, and you think about whether or not it's aimed at you. I can't think of a better way to be." He kissed her cheek. "I do enjoy being married to you, Kate Whitaker."

She rested her head on his shoulder. "I love being married. I don't have to make all decisions by myself. Your mother and I are splitting the housework, so neither of us feel overwhelmed. I think we've got a good arrangement."

He rested his cheek atop her head. "Not to mention having wonderful friends to spend time with. Are you really going to get a sewing machine tomorrow?"

She nodded. "I am. I'll get so much more done with one, and I could drop the prices on my dresses a little because it won't take me nearly as long as it has to get things done."

"I think that's very smart of you," he said. "But don't drop your prices. People come to you expecting quality and uniqueness. If you drop your prices, you won't make as much, and people will think your dresses aren't as good as they have been."

Kate thought about what he'd said for a moment before nodding. "All right. I'll keep them at the same price."

"Now that you're getting along with my mother better, are you still going to go into town to work every day?"

She nodded. "Unless she needs me for something here. I think it's better if I'm not always under her watch, if that makes sense."

Emmett nodded. "I think that's very wise. And I may still fix up that cabin. Then you or mother can use it if you want to. And we can have guests stay in it."

"If you want to."

"I do. I think Mother needs us with her right now as she grieves for Father, but it won't always be that way, and she'll want her own space."

"All right!" Kate liked the idea of being able to escape as well. "Do you like to build?"

He nodded. "I like most things I can do with my hands."

"So doing the ranch's books isn't at the top of your list?"

He chuckled. "I'd rather cut my hand off."

She giggled. "But you'll do it anyway because it's your job."

"Yes, I will. But it won't be easy."

THE FIRST THING KATE did when she got to town the following morning was to go and purchase her sewing machine. She was so excited to get back to the dress shop and learn to use it, she didn't notice all the people looking at her while she was in the store.

She did notice when women stopped her and apologized for the way they'd talked about her. It was a surprise to think that there were people who actually listened to the pastor and saw themselves in his sermon.

By the time she returned to her dress shop after purchasing the sewing machine, eight different women had apologized to her. "I'll be by later to look at your designs," one of the women said.

Kate smiled. "I look forward to that. We'll find the perfect design for you!"

The machine was delivered just as she got back, and it was set up for her. The beautiful object invited her to sit in front of it. She took a small scrap of fabric, not even big enough for a quilt piece, and folded it over. Her feet moved the treadle as she moved the fabric along under the needle.

Pulling it out, she saw the seam was perfectly straight and perfect. She rubbed her hands together with a gleam in her eye. She wanted to make Julie's dress and have it done before she went home that night. As she had yet to even cut the fabric, she knew it was a big job that would need to be done, but she felt up for it.

That whole day, she cut, sewed, and basted. Working through lunch, she decided to add a small butterfly to the collar of this one. Surely Julie would appreciate the effort.

She finished it just before time to head back to the ranch, hoping her efforts would be met with approval. It felt strange to make something for her mother-in-law when she'd been so cruel, but Kate would make sure everything was done as well as she could. There'd been an apology, and it had seemed heartfelt. Kate was determined to forgive and love with all her heart.

When she arrived home, she had the dress in a bag that she immediately carried upstairs.

In the kitchen, she found Julie alone. "Where's Jesse?" she asked.

Julie turned around, and Kate could see there was dirt on the other woman's nose. They had certainly worked hard all day. "He's napping.

We had a late lunch after planting all morning, and he is exhausted. Poor thing."

Kate smiled. "Thanks for letting him help today. I'm sure he had a wonderful time."

Julie's face lit up. "We both did. I dug the holes and dropped the seeds, and he covered them up. He needs a bath soon..."

"I'm sure he does. I'll probably need to wash his sheets as well."

Laughing, Julie said, "I thought about how dirty he'd make the sheets when I put him in bed, but he couldn't stay awake another moment. He was asleep before I even left his room. I managed to get his shoes off, but that was all."

"At least you did that." Kate rubbed the back of her neck. "I got my sewing machine today, and I have to say, it made things so much easier!"

"I'm happy for you! Do you want to set the table for me?"

When Emmett got home after working all day, he stopped on the porch to listen to his mother and his wife just chatting like normal people. He thanked God that Kate was so forgiving. He wasn't sure he'd have been the same way after all she'd been through.

He stepped into the house after removing his mud-caked boots. "Everyone sounds happy in here."

Kate looked at him, her face absolutely glowing. "I got my sewing machine today, and I love it. I thought it would be hard to learn to use it, but it wasn't at all."

Emmett nodded. "That's wonderful! I'm glad it was so easy. Please tell me you let the store deliver it!"

"I paid a little extra, and they even set it up for me. All I had to do was thread it and start sewing. I think my legs will be sore from using the treadle all day, but soon I'll be used to that."

"Jesse and I got the kitchen garden planted," Ma said. "It was so fun to work with him and watch him concentrate as he made sure each seed was covered."

"So you're done with all the planting?" he asked, surprised.

"Well, I still have to do the second half of the garden. When I put him down for a nap, I slept for a little while as well. It was hard work."

He chuckled. "Sounds like everyone worked hard today. I spent the day in the cabin, making sure the fireplace wasn't blocked and the windows open and close. It'll be ready for use soon."

"That's wonderful!" Kate said.

After that, Julie was quiet. She finished supper while Kate went upstairs to get Jesse. "It's time for supper," Kate whispered to her sleepy son.

Jesse blinked a few times and grabbed Kate by the neck, hugging her. "I had the best day, Mama."

"That's what your grandma told me. I'm glad it was fun."

"So fun!"

They joined the others downstairs and all sat at the table for supper. Emmett's prayer thanked God for giving them the ability to do all they had.

Chapter Nine

After finishing the supper dishes, Kate hurried up to the room she shared with Emmett and got the dress she'd made that day. She smoothed it the best she could without an iron, not wanting her surprisee to be spoiled.

She carried the dress down to the parlor, where she knew her mother-in-law would be, and held it up in front of her. "What do you think?"

Julie looked at it, smiling. "Is that the color my dress will be?" she asked.

"This *is* your dress. I worked all day on it, hoping to surprise you."

"You did it that quickly?"

"I worked through my lunch, and I had the new machine. It still took a lot of very fast stitching, but I wanted to have it done for you today. Then you have plenty of time for alterations if I didn't get your measurements just right." Though she knew it would fit based on the measurements she'd taken, Kate didn't want to sound prideful. "Do you want to try it on?"

Julie nodded. "Yes, I'd like that. You should make yourself a new dress for the benefit as well."

"I...I can't go to a benefit."

"Why not? You're a Whitaker now, and this family has a history of being one of the most prominent families in Cheyenne society."

"I don't think it's a good idea," Kate said. She was certain to be laughed out of the event.

Julie frowned. "You're my daughter-in-law now. No one is going to say anything."

"I think you are underestimating what four and a half years of being treated like a pariah has done to my reputation. I should stay home with Jesse. You and Emmett go."

"But I want my friends to get to know the real you. Please."

Kate wanted to make Julie happy, but she was certain if she went, it would be a bad experience for both of them. "Perhaps a small luncheon or something. I don't think I can jump right into this."

Julie sighed. "And this is all because of the talk I started about you. You have no idea how sorry I am. I saw you as one thing and one thing only, and you are a good mother and a wonderful seamstress. You genuinely care about people. How could I have been so cruel?"

"We'll just have to ease me back into society slowly. It's not a major thing."

"Yes, it is!" Julie shook her head. "When I first saw it was you who had married Emmett, I was certain my life was over. Now I'm begging you not to let your life be over."

Kate smiled. "My life isn't over. It's just starting. I'm newly married. I have a wonderful three-year-old son. I have a mother-in-law who supports me. My business is going well. I'm happy with my life. I don't feel the need to be at all the parties in town."

"But you should have the option to go, and you don't."

Kate shrugged. "If it mattered to me a great deal, then I'd say that. Once I thought it was the most important thing in life. Now, I don't really care. Why would I want to risk being treated poorly by people who have never accepted me for who I am? It doesn't make sense for me to want to put myself into that situation."

Emmett had come in behind Kate, and she hadn't realized it. "Perhaps you could introduce her to a friend or two. Have a luncheon here at the house and invite people you think will be most accepting of Kate. Eventually, I want her to be able to go to events like you're talking about with me, but for now, I think it best if we ease her in slowly. We could even ask the Weatherbys to help."

Julie nodded. "I'll invite a few friends for lunch on Saturday. Do you think Florence would come to support you?"

Kate nodded, smiling. "I know she would. I'll have lunch with her tomorrow and ask her."

"Thank you!" Julie said. "I'll invite threeother women. We'll keep the numbers even. Maybe I'll make it a regular Saturday lunch with new people coming each week. Then you can eventually join the rest of us at evening events sometime soon."

"I think that's wonderful, Mother. And I know Kate will help in any way she can," Emmett said.

"I certainly will. Now, try this dress on. I want to see you in it."

Julie took the dress and disappeared upstairs. Kate looked at Emmett and thanked him. "I don't think she would have given up if you hadn't intervened," she said. "I am not ready to be presented to society in any way. It was bad enough when my parents did that when I was sixteen."

He grinned. "We'll take our time and let you take the lead. It's not worth you worrying about how people will treat you." He put his arms around her and kissed her softly. "Besides, I want you all to myself for a while yet."

She smiled, snuggling against him. "I figured I'd marry a dirt farmer, and here I am, surrounded by people who want me to be part of society. It would be good if I could do it as slowly as I want."

"And you can. If Mother tries to force you to do it too quickly, all you have to do is let me know."

Kate looked toward the door as Julie stood in it, her dress fitting her perfectly. "Oh, you look beautiful!" Kate hurried over and pulled at the dress in a few places, making sure it fit properly. "How does it feel?"

"Scandalous," Julie said. "I don't think I should be wearing anything but black for a while yet."

"You said the event wasn't for a month. Wear black until then. If you need another black dress or two, I can make them as well."

"I don't believe I'll need that but thank you. I do really love this dress."

Jesse had been quietly playing with his wooden train on the floor through all the conversation. He glanced up, and his eyes grew wide. "I have the prettiest grandma in the whole world!"

Julie laughed. "I don't know about that, but I thank you for the compliment." She turned toward the steps. "I don't think alterations are necessary, but I'll go change back into my black dress."

Emmett grinned at Kate. "You just made a beautiful dress for someone who has been gossiping about you for years. I don't think I've ever known anyone who could be so forgiving. I did a good job choosing a wife, didn't I?"

Kate smiled. "Not as good as I did choosing a husband."

THE NEXT COUPLE OF weeks were busy on the ranch and in Kate's dress shop. Emmett put all his time into getting ready for the branding party with a bit of his mother's help. This wasn't a society party, but it was, instead, a party for anyone who wanted to come and help with the castration of the young steers who would then be sold at the market in the fall.

While he was doing that, Kate was dealing with a constant stream of customers in and out of her small shop, each woman wanting a different design, and getting excited about what Kate had to offer.

It was as if everyone was almost accepting her as an equal now, and as much as Kate had thought she wanted it, she wasn't certain that she did. Being a prominent member of society had been important to the younger woman she'd been, who had planned a beautiful extravagant wedding with her mother's help.

She had been quite happy with the small wedding she'd had with Emmett. She hadn't needed half of Cheyenne to see her speak her vows to be married.

The sewing machine was completely changing her work. Everything was done in half the time, but she was getting more orders than ever, so she felt as if she'd never catch up anyway.

When it was time for the branding party, she had a new dress she'd made to wear. While the men worked rounding up the steers and branding and castrating them, the women would work to cook a huge meal for them all to share once the real work was done.

She'd made a stylish dress for herself, but she'd used gingham instead of silk, making it a dress that was practical for work on the ranch. She'd also taken a bit of time to make two huge aprons, which would cover most of the dress for her and Julie. They would be doing most of the cooking, so they would need to be covered well.

Julie had thought ahead and hired a young lady who was the daughter of one of the ranchers who would be helping out. She would watch the small children, while the women cooked and the men took care of the cattle.

Julie had decided to make a few briskets for everyone along with baked beans, and Kate had made a huge potato salad. They'd made thirty loaves of bread for the event, getting up well before the sun so the loaves would be fresh.

The other women helped to cut up the bread and took care of tasks like pulling tables out of the barn that were just for this one meal every year.

It was a long hard day for the men who worked, but equally as hard for the women who fed them. When the last calf was castrated, there was a yell of victory and then all the men washed their hands and faces and went to the area where the food was being served. Each woman had been given a table to serve, and they were all rushing around to make sure there was enough food on their table.

Julie had decided to serve tea, both sweet and unsweet, and let the men tell them which they preferred.

After all the men had two helpings of everything, the women each grabbed a plate and sat at another table entirely. As always for events like these, there were four times as many men as women.

Kate let out a breath. "That was a lot of work. I'd forgotten just how much went into a branding party."

Julie smiled. "I won't be in charge of them forever, but if you need me, I will always be here to help."

Kate smiled. "Thank you."

As all of the women ate the food they'd been cooking since the previous day, there were smiles all around. "I think we made enough food," Julie said. "I was worried about that for a while when I saw how many men came to help." She looked at Mrs. Cooper from the next ranch to their east. "You're next, right?"

Mrs. Cooper nodded. "And I sure would appreciate it if you ladies would help."

"You know we will," Kate said. "The best part about ranching is having all your neighbors helping for branding."

After the meal, the men sat talking at the tables while the women washed all the dishes they'd just dirtied. There was a little brisket left they could have for their lunch the next day, but the beans and potato salad were completely gone. And there was one lone loaf of bread.

They set up two washing stations right out on the lawn and Julie washed the dishes in one of them while Kate took the other. The other women wiped the plates dry and stacked them nicely, so they could just be carried inside and put away.

With so many helping, the dishes were done in no time. Kate was impressed at how efficient the women were, but she knew a lot of it was because of Julie. She'd done this so many times over the years that she knew just the right way to do everything. Kate was happy to be able to learn from her.

They all fell into bed exhausted that night, and though Kate was physically exhausted, her mind was on when she would be in charge of planning the whole party. "Were you happy with how today went?" she asked Emmett.

He nodded. "We got the work done. It was a long day, but the food was good. I really liked your potato salad. My mother insists a potato salad needs pickles, but I was thrilled with how good yours was. I've never been a fan of pickle juice all over everything."

"I'm not either. Jesse loves pickles though. I think Sally did a great job with the small children too."

"It was a good day overall," he agreed. "Did it bother you that Ma took the lead on it and you just had to do what she said?"

Kate laughed softly. "It takes a lot to bother me. I thought it worked out perfectly. We got so much done, and we had plenty of help with the dishes and the serving. No, I want your mother to teach me to be that efficient about everything."

"I'm really proud of how you treated my mother when we were first married. I thought she was going to strangle you at one point, but you just kept smiling at her, and eventually won her over."

"I had nothing to do with it really," she said. "Jesse won her over. He was determined that he would have a grandmother who did things with him and who he could love. He wore her down."

"He did at that." Emmett sighed. "Have you thought about us having children at all?"

"I would love for us to have children together. I think your mother would dote on them. She already dotes on Jesse, and he's not even technically hers."

"Do you want many children?" he asked.

"I've always wanted to have as many children as God would allow. It would be nice to have a little boy who looked just like his father."

"I was thinking about a girl who looked just like her mother." He gathered her close, too tired to do much more than hold her.

"We'll have a half dozen of each and call it good," she said, grinning.

"That would work perfectly for me." Emmett felt relief wash over him. As much as she loved Jesse, he was worried that she wouldn't care to have his children, because she didn't love him like she had Jesse's father.

"For me too!" She smiled in the dark. "And we still have two bedrooms to put them into."

"We do. When Ma moves to the cabin, we'll have even more space."

"Are you sure that's what you want?" Kate asked. "For your mother to move away? She's so good with children that I think it would be good if she stayed."

He sighed. "As long as we can have the bigger room, I'll leave that up to you."

Chapter Ten

By the end of summer, their little family had fallen into a peaceful rhythm. On weekdays, if there was nothing that Julie needed her help for, Kate went into town, leaving Jesse with his grandmother. The two would work in the garden and Jesse would help with whatever Julie asked him to do. He would sleep all afternoon and wake up around the time Kate was coming home from work.

Kate was amazed at how much more business she had than she had before she'd married. Every day she had people stopping in to look at her designs, and most days there were sales.

Florence had her babies, surprising everyone when she had twin girls. Kate had made small dresses for the babies and had presented them to their mother after they'd had lunch together. "You look exhausted!" Kate said.

Florence nodded. "The babies are on opposite schedules. One wants to eat while the other sleeps, and vice versa. I never get to sleep, unless I do it with a baby attached to my breast. Jake keeps saying we should get a wet nurse, but I want to feed my babies."

"Just don't make yourself sick trying to provide them with food. I got sick when Jesse was little, and with no help, it took me forever to get better."

"Thankfully, I have the help I need." Florence shook her head. "I don't know what I'd do without Mrs. Andrews. She's been absolutely a godsend since the day I got here, but even more so now that we have the twins."

Kate nodded. "They sure are little beauties."

Florence smiled. "I agree! What about you? How's business?"

Kate sighed. "There's so much business, I have to make people wait two months for dresses, and that's with my sewing machine. If someone wants something done immediately, I have to charge them extra, and I feel like I'm being rude asking."

"No, that's how business works. I'm sure everyone understands that. Now, for the most important question, how's married life?"

"Wonderful," Kate answered immediately. "Emmett treats me as if I'm the most important person in the world. He tells me I don't need to work unless I want to. He buys me little gifts." Her fingers moved to the cameo attached to the collar of her dress. "He got me this for no reason."

Florence smiled. "He loves you."

"Oh, I'm sure he doesn't. He only married me because I'm the person the matchmaker chose for him."

"I don't think that's true," Florence said. "If that was the case, he wouldn't be buying you little gifts or treating you so well."

Kate pursed her lips. "Maybe that's true."

"It's definitely true," Florence said.

"Julie did say something about how I broke his heart when I got engaged to Jesse all those years ago, but I was sure she had me confused with someone else. It's not possible to break someone's heart if you don't know about it, is it?"

Florence slowly nodded. "He definitely has feelings for you. Question is, how do you feel about him?"

Kate started to shrug, but then she thought better of it. "I...I care about him a great deal, and I love how he plays with Jesse and treats him like his own son. I love *that* part of our marriage." She blushed as she said it because it wasn't something women were supposed to admit to each other. "I...I think I love him. I hadn't ever really thought about it, but if I lost him, I don't know that I could go on."

"You went on after Jesse died."

"I had to. I was expecting."

Florence smiled. "I think there was a lot more to it than that."

"Maybe," Kate said. "I have to get back to work."

"All right." Florence stood and hugged her friend. "Keep thinking about it. You'll know how you feel."

The whole way back to the dress shop, she could think about nothing but Emmett. Did she love him? She had loved him as a friend when they were children, of course, but did she love him as a man?

The thought of spending time with him made her happy. She always looked forward to their evening walks, with or without Jesse. She couldn't imagine growing old with anyone else.

She finished a dress that afternoon before heading home to Emmett and Jesse. As she drove, she had her answer. She loved him. She hadn't tried to fall in love with him, of course. There was no way to make that happen. But the time they'd spent together, and his unwavering support of her had made a huge difference in her life.

When she got home, Emmett was already there, which was unusual. He and Jesse were playing in the yard. Emmett took Jesse's hands and spun in a circle letting his feet fly out into the air. She watched them for a moment, before setting the brake and jumping down.

Emmett looked over his shoulder and saw her, his whole face lighting up. "Well, look who's here!"

Kate walked to her husband, put her arms around him and kissed him. No words were necessary. She just needed him to know she'd missed him.

When she went inside, she stopped at the kitchen. "I'll set the table."

Julie turned to her and smiled. "Thank you."

"Thank you for cooking and taking care of my son."

"Well, he's my grandson," Julie said. "Of course, I'm taking care of him."

"I thank you for that. I love how you've embraced him as if he was your own blood. I know he values his relationship with you."

"I love him as much as if he was my blood, just like I'll love all the babies that come from you and Emmett. Jesse is a very special little boy."

While Kate was setting the table and then mashing potatoes, she thought about her feelings about Emmett. She'd become his wife in every way, and she even had forged a good relationship with his mother. It was hard for her to believe she had because their start had been so rocky, but she valued Julie as she had her own mother.

After supper, Kate did the dishes and then asked Emmett if he wanted to go for a walk to watch the sunset. He grinned. "I'd love to!"

Usually, they gave Jesse the option of accompanying them, but that night, Kate asked Julie to watch him. "Do you mind?"

"Of course not. I think I may give him a bath. He helped me in the garden, which always seems to leave him wearing more dirt than the ground."

"Wait," Emmett said, hurrying upstairs. He came down with something in his hand. He held it out to Jesse, who smiled.

"It's a boat!"

"It is," Emmett said. "I thought it might be fun to play with in the bathtub!"

Jesse rushed at Emmett hugging his legs. "Oh, thank you, Papa!"

As often as Jesse had called Julie Grandma, he had never really called Emmett Papa. Kate's eyes filled with tears as she realized that as much as she had been accepted into this family and felt loved, Jesse had as well. No longer was he the little bastard boy, he was a Whitaker.

"You have fun with Grandma!" Kate said.

"I will! And with my boat!" Jesse ran toward the bathroom with Julie falling behind.

Emmett opened the door, and he and Kate left the house, the two of them holding hands as they walked. "Your mother said something to me once that had me wondering. She said that I broke your heart when Jesse and I got engaged, and that's why you left town."

Emmett was quiet for a moment as he thought about how to answer her. "It is part of the reason I left. In my head, I always planned to marry you, but I never had the nerve to say anything about it."

"Really?" Kate asked, surprised. "I had no idea. None at all!"

"Why would you? You were engaged to him, and you were happy. There was no reason for you to think how your marriage may affect me. I was just a boy you'd gone to school with."

"You're not anymore," she said softly.

"I'm not what?"

"Just a boy I went to school with." She shook her head. "You are so much more to me than that. You're the man who accepted Jesse with no questions asked. You defended me against your mother when she had a problem with our marriage. You make me feel like the most important person in the entire world."

"You are to me," he said, looking down at her. "I probably should have told you before we married that I was in love with you. I've dreamed about coming back, and you decided not to marry, or you were a widow. Any way that you could be the woman waiting for me to come home so we could marry."

"Really?" she asked, stunned. "It took me a little longer than that. Everything you said, everything you've done for me. It all makes me feel loved. I know I must seem a bit dense, but it took me a while to fall in love with you and a little longer to realize I had, but I love you with all my heart, Emmett Whitaker. My life will always be better because you married me."

He stopped walking and took both of her hands in his, looking down into her eyes. "Don't say it if you don't really mean it," he said.

"I do mean it. And I plan to spend the rest of my life showing you how very much I love you and appreciate you. I've known you all my life, and I can say that you've surprised me. I thought I knew all about you, but here you are. I love you, and I don't see that changing anytime soon."

He leaned down and kissed her passionately. "I thought I could spend the rest of my life happy because you were in bed with me every night, but hearing you say those words fills me with a kind of ecstasy I didn't know existed. I love you, and I love Jesse. It doesn't matter if we have a dozen kids of our own. I will still love Jesse as my first."

Together they stood too engrossed in one another to even think about the sunset. When she'd spotted him at the train station, looking for her, she should have known that her life would be better from that moment on.

Epilogue

Kate stood in her newest gown, of her own design of course, waiting for Emmett to pull the sleigh around, so the two of them could go to the annual Christmas party at the hospital. She hadn't wanted to go, but they'd followed Emmett's plan, and she'd gotten to know the society ladies of Cheyenne, two or three at a time, and no one had dismissed her as not being good enough.

Her dress was fitted to her, and showed off her baby bump much better than she would have liked. In two short months, she would be presenting Emmett with his son or daughter, and Jesse with his sibling. It was hard to believe how very much her life had changed since that day in early April when Emmett had stepped off the train and back into her life.

The air was frigid and as soon as she was seated in the sleigh, she pulled the lap robe over them both. The drive to Cheyenne wasn't long, but she was certain they'd both be icicles before they arrived.

"I do hope we're not doing this too soon," she said.

Emmett shook his head. "I think it's time. Time for the whole world to know that I love you with all my heart and that you're a fixture in Cheyenne society for the rest of your life."

Kate snuggled a little closer to him, feeling the heat radiating off his body. "I hope it goes like you think it will," she said.

"You're still worried?" he asked, surprised. "You know Florence and Jake will be there."

"I know. And all the women I've become friends with over the past eight months. I just...I worry they'll still reject me. I spent too many years being the person who was gossiped about by this very group of people."

"Stop worrying. I'm not about to let anyone look down on you."

"I know." She took a deep breath and sat quietly for the rest of the drive, more worried than she should be about what these people would say to her. Not for her anymore though. No, she was worried it would devastate him to realize that no one saw her any differently than they had.

They reached the hospital, and he helped her out of the sleigh, his smile giving her the confidence she couldn't find within herself. "My bag of gifts for the children is in the back," she said.

He had made more boats for the boys at the hospital, and she had found dolls and made them tiny dresses. It had taken a great deal more of her time than she'd realized when she started, but she knew the children deserved them.

Going into the hospital together, she felt her face flushing. What had she been thinking to ask these people to accept her, a woman who had been an unwed mother, as one of their own?

She spotted Florence and Jake off to one side of the room, and with her hand tucked into Emmett's arm, she guided him toward the other couple. "I can't believe I let all of you talk me into this," Kate hissed into Florence's ear.

"It's so good to see you!" Florence said, not acknowledging her friend's words.

"And you!" Kate said, kissing Florence's cheek in greeting.

They were some of the first people there, which made it all that much harder for Kate. If she was going to be rejected, she'd rather it happened immediately, so she wouldn't have to wait.

Instead, a few women gathered around Kate and Florence, greeting them both as if they'd always been part of Cheyenne society. "It's lovely to have you join us, Kate," a woman near their age said. "I'm wearing one of your creations." She spun around quickly so Kate could see her gown.

"And you look lovely in it," Florence said with a smile. "Kate is just a genius when it comes to fabric and finding just the right color for every woman who steps into her shop, isn't she?"

"She is!" the first woman said. "Thank you so much for fitting my dress into your busy schedule. I have a feeling I'll be stopping by in a day or two for more."

Kate smiled. "I'm so glad you like it. I'll happily make you more."

Before she knew what was happening, Kate was surrounded by women who had purchased her gowns. "I hope you're going to hire an assistant soon, because we all need more dresses," one of the women said.

"Are you volunteering?" Kate asked.

Seeing that she was doing more than all right, Emmett kissed her cheek. "I'm going to go put our gifts with the others," he said.

By the end of the night, there was no doubt in anyone's mind that Kate had been accepted back into society. She stood with Florence for most of the night, and the two of them greeted all the other ladies together.

On the drive home, Kate said softly, "Thank you for making me do that. I feel like I've been hiding for no reason."

Emmett said, "You have. And now you don't have to anymore."

"Have I told you I love you yet today?"

"Yes, but you can never say it enough. I love you too."

Settling more firmly against him in the sleigh, Kate knew that her new life was just what she'd needed.